danger.com

@6//Bad Intent/

First Aladdin Paperbacks edition April 1998

Aladdin Paperbacks
An imprint of Simon & Schuster
Children's Publishing Division
1230 Avenue of the Americas
New York, NY 10020

Library of Congress Cataloging-in-Publication Data
Cray, Jordan.
Bad intent / by Jordan Cray. — 1st Aladdin Paperbacks ed.
p.   cm. — (Danger.com ; 6)
Summary: In order to increase his own status at Bloomfield High and win the affection of a pretty, popular cheerleader, Brian, the seemingly mild-mannered class president, allows his secret online identity to develop into something self-serving and dangerous.
ISBN 0-689-81477-1 (pbk)
[1. High schools—Fiction. 2. Murder—Fiction. 3. Computers—Fiction. 4. Popularity—Fiction. 5. Schools—Fiction.]
I. Title. II. Series: Cray, Jordan. Danger.com ; 6.
PZ7.C85955Bag   1998   [Fic]—dc21   97-45010
CIP   AC

danger.com

@6//Bad Intent/

by
jordan.cray

Aladdin Paperbacks

VISIT US ON THE WORLD WIDE WEB
www.SimonSaysKids.com/net-scene

///prologue

Notes from the Underground: The "Water Fountain" at Bloomfield High, an in-school cyber message board area.

Subj: *Media Hounds*
Date: *Monday*
From: *LoneLobo*

Attention, discount shoppers: The media blitz is upon us again. The trial of our very own Wolverine team members on Murder One charges is coming up. And instead of keeping a low profile, Lobo sees guyz breaking out those tight Levi's and grrlz waving those mascara wands. Do you think if you give Yet Another Quote about how A Few Bad Apples Don't Soil a School's Rep that somebody might notice you and make you a Star? Dream on, fellow hounds. Let Coach Cappy R.I.P.

I have a proposal. Let's get radical. Ignore the photographers. Love your hair, but cut the vogue action. Try a little dignity on for size. Let's bring Ye Olde Bloomfield High back to the glory it once had. A school with a rep for cliques, snobs, and phonies. Not *murderers*. We gotta have some *standards*. And that's showbiz, folks.

1//model school, perfect town

When the bell rang, everyone slammed their books closed, even though Mr. Langton was still talking. Bloomfield High is known for its excellent sports teams and the array of expensive cars in its parking lot. Not scholars.

"Finish Chapter Five by Wednesday!" Mr. Langton yelled. "I mean it!"

My best friend, Mal Bouchard, headed over to my desk. We always walk to the cafeteria together. Mal is six feet five inches and he looms over the other students. Since Bloomfield is a major sports school, I bet you're thinking that Mal is on the basketball team.

Wrong! Mal is so uncoordinated that he could trip over a speck of dust, then crash down a full flight of stairs. Every millimeter of those six feet five inches screams, *Geek!*

"So, did you read Lobo's posting this morning?" Mal asked me as we started out of class.

"The guy has a point," I said. "My personal hard drive is going to crash from media overload. If I read another article about 'What's Wrong with Our Kids?' or 'Hidden Horror at Model School' I'll lose the lunch I haven't even eaten yet. We're the Homicidal High School poster child. I didn't even *like* Coach Cappy. Nobody did."

"Turn down the volume," Mal said nervously, looking around. "The president of the student body should never say anything negative about a teacher."

"Relax," I said sourly. The Malmeister is my best bud, no question. He is there for me through thick and thin. As my campaign manager, he guided me through three successful student council elections. Because of his genius, last year I was the first junior ever elected student council president. But sometimes, he forgets to take off his campaign manager hat. If I say anything remotely negative about Bloomfield, he tells me to zip it up.

"I've been asking around," Mal said in a low tone, as if we were students in China discussing democracy. "All the kids agree with Lobo. He's touched a nerve. As usual. We can use this."

"How?" I asked as we headed toward the cafeteria line. Sometimes, I swear I can hear those computer clicking noises coming from Mal's brain. He has a long, mournful face like a hound dog with major mange, and his complexion has its problems. He also has a tendency to hunch his shoulders and lope, instead of walk upright like a Homo sapien. But his brain is awesome.

"Hold on." Mal can never concentrate when food is in the picture. We got in line at the cafeteria and loaded up on lasagna and salad. Mal added two blueberry muffins to his tray.

I looked at him with disgusted awe. "I only had a bagel for breakfast," he complained, grabbing two cartons of chocolate milk.

You know how oceanographers call the great white shark an eating machine? They've never met Malcolm Bouchard.

We sat at our usual table by the window

overlooking the quad. It was still early fall, and lots of kids had taken their sandwiches outside. This way, Mal could see almost the entire senior class without even turning his head. He likes to keep an eye on the action at all times.

"I'm thinking of a new slogan," he said, chewing on a huge forkful of lasagna. Mal always talks with his mouth full. His favorite activities are talking and eating, so why not combine them? "Something like 'Move On.' We need to distance ourselves from the incident."

"It wasn't an incident, it was a murder," I said. "Four of our football players shot their coach, remember?"

"Shhh," Mal said. And with a mouthful of food, you can bet some of it sprayed out. I leaned back to avoid the particle shower. "It's an *unfortunate incident* that was in no way a reflection of the high standards of Bloomfield High," Mal said, pointing his fork at me.

"I've got it down, Mal," I said. "But it's going to be harder to say it when the trial starts."

I should fill you in on what happened in our town, Cicada Heights, last year.

The story goes to prove that you can take a handful of boys, pump them full of macho slogans like "Go For It!" and "No Pain, No Gain!", and they'll turn into a pack of rabid wolves.

Basically, four of our all-American football players from the champion Bloomfield High Wolverines went crazy last year. They woke up, pounded their chests, splashed themselves with *eau de testosterone,* and proceeded to torture a handful of their fellow students.

They formed a secret gang called the 24 Point Club. Nobody ever figured out what the name means, exactly, and the guys aren't talking. On the advice of their very expensive lawyers, so far they've kept their mouths shut.

Here's how it worked. They'd pick a victim, usually a girl. First, they'd steal a personal object, like a glove or a notebook. Then they'd dye it black and send it to the victim with a note, saying, **SOMEDAY YOU WILL DIE,** and signed the 24 Point Club.

At first, it just seemed like a sick prank. But then Denise Samarian was surrounded in the woods one night and frightened so badly, she took off across an icy pond and fell in. No one came to help. She could have drowned, or died of hypothermia, but she got herself out and into her car and drove home with the heater blasting.

Jenny Rigorski was menaced by a group of boys wearing ski masks. Luckily, her father came home before Jenny freaked completely. But then while Megan Malone was baby-sitting one night, she was tormented by threatening phone calls. She bundled three-year-old Tyler in her car and took off, crashing into some bushes. No one was hurt, but the investigation turned serious. Put a little kid in danger, and suddenly, everybody gets upset.

Principal Bigelow called about five emergency meetings of the student council and made a bunch of speeches asking anyone with information to come forward. But for once, even the buzzing Bloomfield High gossip mill was silent. Nobody had a clue who these guys were.

Except Coach Cappistrano, whom everyone called Cappy. He was the coach of the football team, and not the most swift of individuals. But, in the gym locker room, he found a printout of an e-mail message arranging a meeting. He told the assistant coach that he was suspicious because there were no names on the note, only numbers—the note was headed by the figure 2. It was directed to 8, 9, 3, and 4. He thought maybe it was code for the 24 Point Club. He was going to show up at the meeting and try to talk the guys—whomever they were—into giving themselves up.

Coach Cappy went to the rendezvous point, a parking lot in a park outside of town that had an outdoor swimming pool, so nobody went there in winter. Apparently, all the Wolverine football heroes were already there—Greg Littlejohn, Kyle Woodham, David Rollins, and Jamie Fletcher.

Nobody knows what the coach said, or what happened. Because they were the last people to see him alive.

Coach Cappy went back to his house. Later that night, the doorbell rang. He answered it. The next thing Cappy knew, he had an extra nostril. Right between the eyes.

At first, it seemed like a random, shocking act in a town that hardly bothers to keep crime statistics. We thought of crime as something that happened in Chicago, an hour away. Then the cops found the e-mail in Cappy's car, and the assistant coach told them that the last time he'd seen him, the coach was heading to a meeting with the 24 Point Club.

The cops did some pretty impressive TV show forensic work. Casts were taken of the tire tracks on Coach Cappy's lawn. And two footprints were found. One was of an expensive athletic shoe. The other was even more distinctive. They traced it to a company that makes custom-made hiking boots and keeps records of people's measurements. That led them to Jamie Fletcher. Listen, if you're going to commit murder, buy your shoes at Kmart.

The tire tracks matched Kyle's Jeep. A tiny spot of Cappy's blood was found on David's sweatshirt. Greg's Nikes matched the other print.

The boys were arrested. The gun was never found. The evidence was circumstantial, but it all added up to a big neon Guilty sign.

None of the guys would talk except to say that they had formed the club, and things had gotten out of control. They were sorry about that, but they claimed to know nothing about Cappy's murder. Sure, they'd been to his house a bunch of times. And when he'd shown up at the parking lot, he'd had a nosebleed, and it had gotten on David's sweatshirt. But murder? No way.

All Kyle, Jamie, David, and Greg said was, *Maybe things got out of hand,* and, *I guess some of us used bad judgment.*

The district attorney didn't file Bad Judgment charges. He filed Murder One.

Shock rippled through our town. Nobody could believe that our beloved athletes could do such a thing. And there was even some grumbling in town about how fast the cops had moved. Couldn't they have waited until *after* football season? They put the championship in jeopardy!

Cicada Heights is an oasis of rationality

and high-mindedness in a world of trivialities.

We have more golf courses than churches, and more plastic surgeons than grocers.

Even after a pileup of evidence that could be floated out to sea on a barge, some kids still don't believe any of the players did it. Greg's old girlfriend, Talia Wilson, *still* wears her "Totally Innocent" T-shirt.

Things got worse when the media got wind of the story. At first, when the reporters showed up, everyone was totally impressed. All the students were dying to be interviewed, and some guy from the *New York Times* even lived here for six months to research a book.

Up till then, Bloomfield High had been a major model school. Smack in the middle of upper-middle-class suburbia, Bloom High boasts every perk a high school student can possibly crave—computer labs, swimming pool, athletic fields, million-dollar football stadium, in-school TV studio. The school itself, which was built in the thirties, has been completely modernized. A new wing was added just ten years ago, with a system of enclosed catwalks linking the two buildings.

After the arrests, a black cloud seemed to descend on the school. We told the world that the boys didn't represent Bloomfield High. That we were full of moral, upstanding young citizens. But nobody seemed to believe us.

Except us.

2//black cloud

"Hey," Mal said, waving a muffin in my face. "Let's keep our eye on the ball, bud. Never mind the trial. Let's concentrate on the election." He popped half the muffin into his mouth.

"Okay. What do you have in mind?" I asked.

But Mal shushed me again. This time, he sprayed muffin crumbs on my shirt.

I was about to protest, but Mal pointed his chin toward Emily Talladega, who was bearing down on us. I clammed up. Not that Emily was a big gossip, but she was my major academic rival, so I wasn't about to reveal any campaign secrets.

Mal and I used to be classified in the same Geek Pool as Emily, but we've achieved special status due to our stunning student council successes. Emily is my main competition for valedictorian this year. Everybody likes Emily. She's a credit to our school. Our competition is totally friendly.

In her dreams.

"Greetings," Emily said as she came up. "How's the campaign going?"

Mal's mouth was full, so he just grunted.

"Okay," I said. "We've got it covered."

"You must be worried now that Jason Polemus entered the race," Emily said. She tucked her flyaway brown hair behind her ears. Sometimes her big brown eyes reminded me of a sick cow.

Mal swallowed. "We are not worried about Jason Polemus. He's just a football player."

Emily rolled her eyes. "There's no such thing as *just* a football player at Bloomfield High. Jason is hero material."

I looked at Mal. Maybe Emily had a point. In any other venue, he'd be a cute, dim-looking guy with dimples and curly hair. But in our town, baby boys are given a football at birth. Our high school games are televised and most of the time make the front page of the town paper. Sometimes, we even make the Chicago papers.

Last year, Jason was just a second-string quarterback. He was not the most athletically gifted guy. He didn't date the hottest cheerleaders. Nobody carried him on their shoulders after a game.

Then the four best players were arrested right before the play-offs, and Jason was moved up to first string. He still wasn't very good. But he tried hard. He'd squeak by with a touchdown at the last minute, or fumble a snap and then dive headfirst to cover it. And to everyone's surprise, we won two games.

He brought back pride to Bloomfield, just when we thought our black cloud was permanent. We didn't win the championship, but for the first time in Bloomfield High history, nobody cared. Jason played his heart out, and that was all that mattered. He was a hero in all our hearts.

He's a dim-witted, muscle-bound ape.

"I hear his parents are on his case," Emily told us. "His academic record isn't exactly stellar—and he's not about to get a football scholarship. They don't give them for being a good sport. They want him to get into a good college, so they're pushing him toward student government. I mean, let's face it. What does Jason have going for him besides popularity?"

"Athlete's foot?" I suggested.

Mal smirked.

"Well, his parents are smart," Emily went on.

Mal snorted. "There goes that genetic inheritance theory."

"I mean, he does need something. So you're not worried about him?" Emily's soft brown eyes peered at me. I almost expected her to moo. "Because if you need help, I—"

"We don't need help, Emily," Mal snapped. "It's under control."

"Oh. Okay." Emily looked hurt. "Well, I'd better go eat, I guess."

We watched her make her way back to her table in the "nowhere" section of the cafeteria. Emily has rather large feet, and she is fond of wearing white athletic shoes with her skirts. It's not the most attractive combo.

Her friend Heidi Huberman sat waiting. Nobody sits with Emily and Heidi. If it is possible to look more pathetic than Emily, Heidi somehow achieves it. She is tall and thin and has a truly long neck. If the girl wears a spotted dress, she is in serious danger of being mistaken for a giraffe.

"I think you hurt her feelings, bud," I told Mal.

"Yeah, I can tell you're concerned," Mal said. "That girl has a wicked crush on you, bud. Do I smell *eau de romance* in the air?" Then he leaned over and mooed in my ear. *"Moooooo!"*

I swatted at his head. "You smell *eau de jerk*," I said. "Emily Talladega is way down the food chain, bud."

Okay, you're thinking Mal and I are pigs, right? We compare girls to cows and giraffes, we rank them, and we make fun of them. And if you could see us in person, you'd be wondering how we have the nerve.

Because, like Emily Talladega, I am no example of the triumph of human genetics. I'm skinny. I wear glasses. I've got brown hair and brownish eyes. I'm the kind of guy who people have to think about two or three times before they remember who I am. And then, they forget.

But haven't you heard of the human chain of pain? Guys like Mal and me *need* others to look down on. It helps us deal with our lack of self-esteem and our developing sense of self.

Or maybe we're just mean.

"Don't look so down," Mal said, chomping on his salad. "It's not too late to turn back the Jason tide. We need to take a major bull session on Friday night to get the ball rolling. I've got plans."

"I can't believe you're taking the Jason thing seriously," I said. "The guy is a lightweight."

"He's a lightweight with dimples," Mal said. "I have two words for you. Dan Quayle. He was vice president of the entire *country,* bud."

"Okay, okay," I said. "You're the boss. What plans are we talking about?"

Mal chewed thoughtfully for a moment. "I wonder if we could get an endorsement from LoneLobo? He's an opinion-swinger."

"But nobody knows who he is," I protested. I pushed away my orange drink. Why had I ordered orange drink with lasagna? It was a totally gross combination. Maybe I'd hung around Mal too much. I was starting to pick up his eating habits.

"I could probably figure out a way to find out who he is. All I have to do is put the brain cells to work on it," Mal said. "The guy's a complete jerk, but people listen to him."

"You think Lobo is a jerk?" I asked, startled. Lobo is the coolest guy at Bloomfield High, and that's saying something. LOBO RULES! graffiti is constantly Now Showing at a Bathroom Near You. "You never said that before."

"He's wind passed in a grocery bag," Mal said, slurping down his chocolate milk. "He makes me wonder about the average IQ of our soon-to-be alma mater. But I always wonder about that. The point is, he *unites* us. Everybody thinks he's cool. And at this school, that's a miracle. Everybody hates everybody else. The jocks hate the brains, who make fun of the geeks, who look down on the nerds, who pick on each other."

"I say forget it," I said, pushing away my tray. "Trying to find out who Lobo is would be a major waste of time not to mention impossible. Let's talk posters. That's what'll get me reelected." My gaze panned over the cafeteria, and my internal gearshift suddenly stuck on one perfect image. "So start accessing those propaganda . . . uh . . . skills, bud—"

Mal made a siren noise. "This is a test of the emergency broadcast system. This is only a test." He smirked. "So what is Dawn Sedaris wearing today? Fill us in on the habits of the fashion forward, Brian."

I shrugged. "I didn't notice."

A short skirt in a heathery green print, a white T-shirt, and a green suede vest. Knee-high black suede boots. Green tights. And I thought I saw the glint of those dangling earrings she wears. I asked her once what the stones were. *Peridot,* she'd said. I still remember the small explosion of air against my cheek as she'd made the "p" sound.

"You've got it bad, bud," Mal chortled.

"You're insane," I said.

"No, you're insane," Mal countered. "If you think that a walking vision like Dawn Sedaris would ever take you seriously."

"We're friends," I said.

Mal snorted. "Right. She lets you hold her spotlight. That makes you really close."

Dawn and I are both in the Bloomfield Players, the drama club. An appreciation of the arts is the goal of every well-rounded student.

I joined for the girls.

Have you ever noticed that the best-looking girls join the drama club in every school? Since I'm basically talentless, I volunteered to work the lights. Dawn had the lead in the play they were doing, and the thought of staring at her for hours at a time was not exactly unpleasant.

"Let me clue you in on something, bud," Mal said. He opened his second carton of chocolate milk. "Girls like Dawn Sedaris have a ranking system encoded in their heads. She'd never consider you seriously. She has everything she needs for major star wattage. Designer clothes, money, dates, friends. Girls like that never cross over and date guys like us. They use us. They ask us for favors, and we do them. We loan them our class notes. We tutor them. We fix their hard drives. But we don't date them. Just wait."

"Maybe that's true about other girls," I said. I couldn't let this one go by. "But Dawn's different. We're friends. We talk all the time."

"Let me guess," Mal smirked. "Do you talk about *your* hopes and dreams? What you think, what *you* feel? Or do you talk about Dawn?"

Well. We did mostly talk about Dawn. About how she did in rehearsal, about how she should direct her future career path. Was modeling a good idea, or should she go into fashion design? Very deep stuff.

"We don't talk about her all the time," I lied. "We talk about me, too."

"Looks like you'll get your chance to discuss the endless fascinating facets of Brian Rittenhouse, then," Mal murmured.

And suddenly, Dawn was standing there. At my very own cafeteria table.

Her blue gaze penetrated my formidable defenses. Her teeth grazed her lower lip.

"Brian? Can I talk to you? You know, *alone?*" Dawn asked meaningfully.

"Step into my office," I said masterfully. Ignoring Mal's major eye roll, I got up and moved down to the other end of the table. I pulled out a chair for Dawn.

She slid into it and leaned forward toward me. Our knees were almost touching.

"Brian, I really need your help," Dawn said. She looked down at her hands. She was embarrassed about something.

"You can tell me, Dawn," I said. "What's up?"

"It's like, you're really smart, okay? And you know everybody at school?" Dawn's voice died away. She had moved here from Tennessee a year and a half ago, and she had this habit of putting a question mark at the end of sentences that weren't questions. It totally charmed me.

"What do you need?" I felt pretty awesome about the compliments. Take that, Malcolm Bouchard! "Name it."

"Well . . . do you think you could help me find out who LoneLobo is?" Dawn blurted.

Seconds ago, I had told Mal there was no way to figure out Lobo's identity. But this time, the person asking me wasn't a geek of my gender.

"Sure," I said.

She smiled, and somewhere in my heart, a love song swelled. Something about blue eyes and one true love. I moved a fraction of an inch closer so that our knees actually made contact.

Then I remembered Mal saying, *Girls like that use us. They ask us for favors, and we do them.*

So even while the love song swelled, a tiny kernel of anger did, too.

3//how to trap a wolf

"Brian? Are you okay?"

"Why do you want to know who he is?" I asked.

Dawn swept back a lock of thick blond hair. "I totally love his sense of humor, okay? He's so ferociously cool. But you know what else?" Dawn leaned closer to me. I caught a whiff of her shampoo, and something happened to all the muscles in my body.

They, like, *dissolved?*

"I think he really, you know, needs a friend?" Dawn said.

I swallowed. "How do you know that?"

"I just *know,*" Dawn said with great intensity. "I *feel* it, okay?"

"So you want to be his friend," I repeated. "Come on, Dawn. You've got plenty of friends."

"Okay. So maybe I have a crush, then." Dawn giggled. "A little crush. Okay, a major crush. But can you blame me, Brian?" Dawn looked deep into my eyes. "I mean, the whole thing with Mark *destroyed* me. I thought I'd never love someone else again."

Mark Skeeter and Dawn dated the first summer she moved here, after sophomore year. They kept up their romance through most of the fall. Then Dawn broke up with him to date Jamie Fletcher. Needless to say, this was before Jamie was arrested. As soon as Dawn found out about the 24 Point Club, she freaked. She went for comfort to Mark, who felt sorry for her, but didn't take her back. Dawn was pretty upset about it at the time.

Mark is editor in chief of the school paper, and an all-around good guy. He won a statewide journalism award last year. You might think he's smart, right? But he rejected Dawn Sedaris, and that makes him a fool.

"You love Lobo?" I asked.

"Well, of course not. I don't even know

him. But I feel like I know his soul, you know?" Dawn said, her eyes shining. "So will you help me?"

Pop. Pop. It was like microwave popcorn exploding. Tiny bursts of anger.

"I don't know, Dawn," I said. "It's not easy to figure out who someone is on the Water Fountain. Where would you start?"

"I don't know," Dawn said impatiently. "That's why I'm asking you." She sighed and put her hand on my knee. "I need you, Brian."

Pop. Pop. Need me for what? To set you up with another guy?

"Be my friend?" Dawn whispered pleadingly.

I carefully wiped my hand on the side of my pants, so that Dawn couldn't see. I covered her hand with my hopefully dry one. "Of course I'll be your friend. Let's go at this logically."

She sat back happily. "I just *knew* you'd know what to do! Logic! You are so ferocious!"

"We should look back at the old Water Fountain postings," I said. "I think we can access back two weeks. We'll scan them and try to pick up clues. What are Lobo's likes and dislikes? Is he a good student, or a bad one? Is he a jock, or is he into music or movies?"

Dawn looked at the clock on the wall. "That sounds fabulous, Bri," she said hurriedly. "Can you do that today? I have to go meet Steffi. We have a free period together, and I promised to help her with her column."

Pop. Pop. Steffi Minor is Dawn's best friend. She writes the gossip column for the school paper. I was mildly annoyed that Dawn would leave me for such an airhead. You'll notice that Dawn didn't go to Steffi to help her figure out who Lobo was.

No, she left that task for dependable Brian.

"I'm really sorry," Dawn said. She must have noticed I wasn't exactly thrilled to have her dump the project in my lap. "I promised Steffi. And you know how she is."

Actually, I didn't. Steffi Minor had never given me more than a big, fake, *Hi, Brian! How's every little thing with you?* before sweeping away without waiting for an answer.

"Sure," I said.

"She has to finish her column every Monday by the end of lunch," Dawn said, rolling her eyes. "They put the paper to bed on Tuesday morning, and she doesn't want to stay any later at school than she has to."

"I hear you," I said, when I really wanted ed to say, *What a complete moron.*

"The funny thing is, she always talks about herself like she's this *serious* journalist?" Dawn said. She lowered her voice. "I happen to know for a fact that Mark can't bring himself to proof her column, okay? He makes Emily do it."

Emily Talladega is the assistant editor of the *Scroll.*

Dawn cocked her head. A twinkle lit up her dark blue eyes. "I saw you talking to Emily before," she said in singsong voice. "You two would make a cute couple."

I discovered for the first time that I could actually be irritated with Dawn Sedaris.

"The chances of that happening lie somewhere in the range of negative numbers," I said.

Dawn giggled. Like most girls, she loved it when boys trashed another girl. Who am

I kidding? Guys loved it when girls trashed another guy, too.

She stood up. "Yeah, well, I never understood why a girl with such huge feet would wear those big white sneakers all the time. I mean, she's supposed to be *smart,* right? Even I'm smarter than that."

"When it comes to fashion, Dawn, you could win the Nobel prize," I said.

"Do they give one for fashion?" Dawn asked, her mouth open. "I didn't know that."

"Absolutely," I assured her. Let Dawn have her dreams. I certainly wouldn't be the one to smash them.

"Cool! So, I'll see you later?" Dawn asked.

"You can count on it," I promised.

She hurried out of the cafeteria. A second later, the lumpy shadow of my best friend loomed over my shoulder. He bent down and spoke right near my ear. "She wanted a favor, right?"

"Not at all," I said, standing up. "She wants to help on the campaign. She said she'd do anything."

Mal's eyebrows raised. "Anything? Will

she be my date for the senior prom? Sit next to me in the back row of the movies?"

"Mal—"

"Use my shower?" Mal asked.

I grabbed my books. "I'll let you know. I have some stuff to take care of."

"Wash my car?" Mal yelled after me.

Mal and I have been friends since fourth grade, when we both got picked last at softball. When you have a friendship with someone that's based on the fact that nobody else wants to be friends with you, there can be a weird vibe at times. Even though you're loyal to each other, you know that basically you're together because there's nobody else out there. And you know the other guy has to put up with whatever you dish out.

So even though I know that Mal would give me the shirt off his back (I'd never wear it—the guy really sweats), I also have to withstand a whole lot of major grief from him. But that's okay. Because I give him major grief, too. It's the cement that makes our friendship strong.

Needless to say, I didn't tell Mal that I was going to wait by Dawn's locker after school that day. I'd only get grief. Mal would lean over and sniff me and say, *Do I detect a whiff of* eau de desperation?

I told him I had a dentist appointment.

The last bell finally rang, and I ran to the fourth floor in the new wing, where Dawn's locker was. I saw her heading down the hall toward me. Good. She was alone. Usually, there is a crowd of girls around her, all giggling and hooting at some deep dark secret that's probably completely lame.

"Hi," I said as she came up. "I accessed the last two weeks of the Water Fountain." I patted my folder. "I have it right here. If you want, we could head to the Crunch Café and grab a cappuccino and look it over. If you want."

I'd never drunk a cappuccino in my life.

"Steffi and I already went over the printout we pulled up," Dawn told me as she twirled her lock. "I told her about my crush. That was a fabulous idea, you know, about looking for clues? We narrowed it down to three suspects."

Talk about *pop!* It is seriously distressing to be confided in, and then find out that you've been aced out by an airhead. Not to mention go to the trouble of printing out postings when you should be working on your reelection campaign.

Dawn didn't notice my annoyance this time. "We circled any references to extracurricular activities or grades. Then Steffi said we should look at his vocab."

"His what?"

"His favorite words, sayings, things like that. For example, he was the one who started everyone saying 'ferocious' and 'love the hair.' And he called cute girls 'tasty cakes' the other day."

"The guy is a poet."

Dawn ignored this. "Steffi pointed out that Kevin Fallows called her 'tasty' just last week—*before* Lobo said it in a posting on the board. Plus, he is incredibly cute."

"It's probably the only word he knows. Kevin Fallows as Lobo? I don't think so." I was disgusted. Kevin is a lamebrain. He's a caveman rubbing two sticks together who keeps missing the spark.

Dawn leaned against the locker next to hers. She looked completely and revoltingly dreamy-eyed. "Then we noticed that Lobo seemed to know what's going on in the Players—he knew that Susie Galluci was being replaced by Amanda Summerson in *Mame* before it was posted. And you know how he always says 'that's showbiz, folks!' So we definitely think that Corey Lax is a possibility."

Corey Lax usually plays the lead in all school productions. He's a huge bag of hot wind with good hair. If he could climb into the mirror, he'd marry himself. "*Corey Lax?* Dawn, hold the phone. You—"

"And the third guy is the weirdest of all," Dawn said. "You're not going to believe this one."

"Try me."

"He's running for president," she whispered.

"Of what? The United States?"

She smacked me playfully on the arm. "No, silly! The student body. Steffi thinks it could be Jason Polemus. Isn't that incredible? I mean, he seems sort of shy, doesn't he?"

I now had a jumbo-sized tub o' popcorn crackling in my brain. A tub so big, you can't finish it, even during a triple feature of *Star Wars*.

"Dawn," I said, "did it ever occur to you that Steffi managed to narrow the field to three of the cutest guys at school?"

Dawn grinned. "Isn't it lucky? I mean, Lobo could have turned out to be a total geek."

She reached in her backpack for her brush and began to run it down her long hair. She caught my eye and she stopped. "I'm not an idiot, Brian. Okay? I *know* Lobo might not be one of those three guys. But it's a place to start."

"I guess," I said dubiously. "But what are you going to do next? Lobo doesn't want to be found out. So you can't just go up to Corey or Kevin and ask him if he's the guy."

Dawn tapped her brush against her palm. "That's true. I guess we have to figure something out? A plan."

"Yeah, well, Steffi seems to be good at this, so—"

She put her hand on my arm. "No. *You*, Brian. I need your help. Please?"

Poppoppopopop Pop! "I don't know," I said, stalling. The chances of my refusing to help Dawn Sedaris were about as great as my chances of developing killer pecs. But the longer I hesitated, the longer she'd keep her hand on my bare forearm. Each little hair was grateful to feel her fingers.

Just then Mrs. Beebe, the assistant principal, caught sight of me. She hurried toward me.

"Brian! Brian! I'm so glad I caught you! Principal Bigelow wants to see you in his office."

"Okay, Mrs. Beebe."

"I mean *now*."

"Oh." I gave Dawn a reluctant look. "Business of state. You know."

"Okay. But you'll think about a plan, right?"

I took her hand and squeezed it. "I'll flush the wolf from his lair, Princess. Promise."

* * *

Principal Bigelow is a hardworking public servant with that special gift of being able to really reach kids. We're proud to have him lead us here at Bloomfield High.

He's a New Age lunkhead.

"Brian, how're you doing? Have a seat." Mr. Bigelow waved me to the seat across from his desk. Then he walked around his desk and pushed the seat next to mine closer.

Uh-oh. It was going to be one of those heart-to-heart chats. I put on my I'm-So-in-Touch-with-the-Student-Body face.

"As you know, Brian, the murder trial is scheduled to start in just a few weeks. Once again, Bloomfield High is going to be under tremendous pressure because of the unfortunate incident last year."

I nodded soberly.

"What you may not know is that a new detective has taken over the case. Detective Hanigan has a theory that the ringleader of the 24 Point Club has never been caught. This boy is holding something over the other boys' heads so that they won't talk. I know it sounds far-fetched, but this

Hanigan is determined to pursue it. Do you remember that number 2 that was on the memo that Cappy—Coach Cappy—Coach Cappistrano found?"

I nodded again.

"Well, Detective Hanigan finds it significant, even though it was never actually *proven* that there could have been another student involved." Bigelow leaned forward. "Grace Hanigan is an alumnus of Bloomfield High, so I'm confident that her loyalty and fair-mindedness will put the issue to rest at last."

"I'm sure that's true, sir," I said.

"Unfortunately, she needs to interview students here," Principal Bigelow continued with a sigh. "It's going to dredge up all that pain again, just when we've dealt with it in the sensitivity sessions I organized. This is a time of healing. Detective Hanigan was sympathetic, but . . . well. We need to open up the dialogue again. We have to revisit the pain, Brian."

He patted back the tufts of gray hair that are usually out of control by ten in the morning. He doesn't get a decent haircut because he is one of those balding guys who thinks no one will notice his hairline if he keeps his hair long on the sides. All of us here at Bloomfield are dreading the day he attempts The Comb-over.

"What can I do to help, sir?" I asked.

"I'm so glad you asked. Keep your hand on the pulse of the student body. Take their temperature. And keep me informed. Can you do that for me, Brian?"

It sounded like a job for Nurse Quincy, not me. But I wasn't about to say that to Principal Bigelow. What did we all learn in spelling class? The principal is your *pal*.

"I totally understand, sir," I said with my decisive prez nod.

"Now, I must tell you, this Detective Hanigan is on a wild-goose chase," Principal Bigelow said. "I just refuse to believe there is another murderer at Bloomfield High. And I think we should all keep an open mind about our other boys on the football team, too."

"I agree absolutely, Mr. Bigelow," I said. *They're guilty as sin.*

He smoothed his hair back again. He

straightened his striped tie. He cleared his throat.

"But, well, just in case there is a killer at Bloomfield High—keep your eyes and ears open."

4//a murderer among us

Let me enlighten you. If you *really* keep your eyes and ears open at Bloomfield High, you'll want to throw up in about three seconds. All you'll see is hair gel, and all you'll hear is, *Awesome!* and, *That is a ferocious sweater, girl!*

So instead of worrying about murderers, I focused on Dawn.

"I've been thinking over your problem," I told her the next morning. I caught up with her outside school and drew her away from the crowd.

Dawn usually hangs in the portion of the quad right by the front steps. Mal calls it The Penthouse. It's where the group we call The Chosen Few hang out.

Early on freshman year, Mal figured out the hierarchy of Bloomfield and gave names to the different groups. There is a subgroup called the Almosts, which consists of kids like Mark Skeeter. They do things like work on the school paper, or sing in chorus, or are on the track team. They are fairly good looking, and they have decent cars, but they have no glamour. Occasionally, exceptional Almosts can cross over and date one of the Chosen Fews.

Then there are the Nevers, people like Emily and Heidi, whom nobody has energy enough to trash but nobody cares about, either. And then there are the Voids, who are so dreadful, they are even beneath the Nevers. They hang out in a region Mal calls the Trailer Park, by the bike racks.

Mal and I solved the problem of where to hang by pretending to be super busy and rushing into school every day. We consider ourselves Above Categorization. We are Cool Geeks.

Before we'd even started high school, Mal told me he'd given a lot of thought to the next four years. His point was that guys like us usually fall through the cracks in high school. They get teased, wedgied, and ignored. "Then, at our twentieth high school reunion, we come back as millionaires, and everybody hits us up for a job," Mal pointed out to me. "But I don't want to wait that long to get a little respect."

"So what's your big idea?" I asked.

"Student government," Mal answered.

Mal decided that I should run for treasurer freshman year. I pointed out that no freshman runs for a student council office. Bloomfield High is a big school. Nobody had ever heard of me. How could I even get noticed? And if I did get noticed, who would vote for me? I might get elected mayor of Nerd City, but that's about it.

Mal just waved his hand. The pimple medicine he'd dotted on his face was shiny in the bright electric light of his kitchen. But his eyes burned with fervor. He was a messiah with acne.

"All you need is spin," he said. "Which I shall provide."

So freshman year, I ran for treasurer. Mal took pictures of every one of my straight-A report cards since first grade and then digitalized them on his computer. Then he printed out a poster with each report card, making a big grid. The slogan read:

**IF YOU CAN'T GET SMART,
GET BRIAN**

I won by a landslide.

Sophomore year, we ran for secretary. Then, for junior year, Mal dropped the bombshell—we were going for the presidency. Nobody thought I could win except Mal. He ran a blitzkrieg campaign, and I demolished the competition, this straight-arrow bore, Dave Wentlow. This year, I was up for reelection. I considered myself a shoo-in. Mal was way too worried about Jason Polemus. He was Dave Wentlow with dimples.

I'd get up to speed on the campaign soon. But first, I had to concentrate on Dawn Sedaris.

"So did you think of anything?" Dawn asked.

I nodded. "I think the best thing to do is flush him out. Write a posting directly to Lobo," I directed. "Tease him a little bit.

Tell him you figured out his identity. If he wants to know more, he can e-mail you. That way, everything still stays basically anonymous. You won't scare him off."

Dawn bit her lip. She has this tiny beauty mark by the left side of her bottom lip, and it disappeared behind her teeth. I missed it.

"But I don't have a computer," she said.

"You don't?" I was surprised. Everyone in Dawn's crowd has a state-of-the-art PC, or carts around some superdeluxe notebook loaded with the latest software.

She shrugged. "I just wasn't interested in cyber stuff until recently. I, you know, haven't had a chance to buy one?"

"No problem," I said. "I can set up an e-mail address for you on my account. Lobo can write you there."

Dawn brightened. "You'd do that for me?"

"In a heartbeat," I said. I gave her a meaningful look. I was sure that the quest for Lobo's identity was bringing us so totally together. Soul mates.

"You're a pal," Dawn said, which was

not exactly the message I wanted to hear. The message I wanted to hear was, *Brian, you are a love god, and I want to be your slave.*

"Will you help me write the posting?" Dawn asked. "And will you check every hour to see if he answers? It's so incredibly crucial. I just have to know who he is." She hesitated. "Brian, there's something else. I know that I've totally intruded on your time and everything? But—"

"I'm here for you, Dawn," I told her.

Her gaze swept the quad. Then she looked back at me and lowered her voice. "Have you heard about this detective? She's interviewing some students. And she wants to interview me."

"You?" I asked, surprised. "How come?"

"Because of *Jamie,*" Dawn said. "Because I was, you know, dating him during . . . that time. Even though I didn't know a thing. I mean, it was a *secret* club, right?"

"So don't worry about it," I said. "The police asked you questions, too, right?"

"And the district attorney," Dawn said,

nodding. "But I don't have to testify or any-thing. Because I don't *know* anything. So why does she want to talk to me?"

"Dawn, don't worry about it," I said. "She probably wants to ask you a couple of questions about Jamie. No big deal. Do you want me to meet her with you?"

She bit her lip again. "No, I don't want to look guilty, you know? I'm just . . . nervous about it. I thought it was all behind me."

"We all did," I said. My gaze swept the quad. I thought about what Principal Bigelow had said. Was there a murderer among us?

The sun shone on the green grass. Someone laughed. I saw a blur of smiles and hair-tossing and heard Susie Galluci's—an Almost—high-pitched giggle. The windows of Bloomfield High sparkled, and the brass handrails gleamed.

High school sure doesn't seem like a set-ting for murder, does it? Bloomfield High is a model school. It just couldn't happen here.

But that's what we'd said last year.

* * *

Subj: *I Know You, Wolfman*
Date: *Tuesday*
From: *newdawn*
To: *LoneLobo*

Sure, reality bites. But do you, Lobo?

I think I have a pretty good idea, but I'd like to know for sure. I want to meet the real you.

If you want to meet me, e-mail me at the above address and set up a time. I'll be there.

Subj: *meeting?*
Date: *tues*
From: *LoneLobo*
To: *newdawn*

So, you think you know the real me. I'm intrigued.

Lobo prefers to run solo, but how can I resist the dawn?

Butler's Lake hut, five p.m., Friday.

Dawn caught up to me outside my chem class. "Did you hear from Lobo?" she asked breathlessly. We had posted on the message board that morning.

I handed her the printout. "He wants to meet you Friday at five P.M."

"This is ferocious," Dawn breathed. Then she suddenly looked like she'd been struck by lightning. "Wait! The game is Friday night! That won't give us much time together."

In Cicada Heights, "the game" is always the Bloomfield High football team.

"To do what?" I asked.

"To talk. I mean, the game starts at seven, and the players have to get there way before," Dawn said, disappointment in her voice. "Maybe that means it's not Jason."

"Dawn, I'm having second thoughts about this," I told her. "Think about it. It will be close to dark then. And the pond hasn't frozen over yet, so no one will be there to skate. It's a pretty isolated spot."

"So?"

"So, I don't know if you should go," I said.

"Of course I'm going to go, Brian," Dawn said. "This is my chance to meet Lobo!"

"Then I'm going with you," I said.

She shook her head. "No way. You'd scare him off."

"Hold the phone a sec," I said. I drew her into an empty classroom. "Dawn, don't you remember? Butler's Lake is where Denise Samarian fell through the ice and almost drowned."

"So?" Dawn said.

"So, did it ever occur to you that it might not be a coincidence that Lobo picked that place?" I pointed out. "Remember that Detective Hanigan still thinks the ringleader of the 24 Point Club is around and laying low. What if it's *Lobo?*"

"That's ridiculous!" Dawn said. "What a stretch. I thought you were the logical one, Brian," she said teasingly.

"So why did Lobo pick the hut at Butler's Lake?"

She shrugged. "Because he wants to be alone with me," she said in a patient tone.

"Look, maybe it's far-fetched," I said. *And maybe I was grasping at straws.* "But don't you think you should be careful?"

"I'm not worried." Dawn smiled. "Anyway, Steffi thinks she figured out who

Lobo is. She's positive it's Kevin. She says Kevin was staring at me in social studies. Plus, he paid for my soda in the cafeteria today."

"Whoa, the clues are piling up," I said.

Dawn hesitated. "You know, Brian, I know you think I'm dumb."

I looked shocked. "I don't think you're dumb!"

And does it really matter if you are?

"I know I'm not the swiftest girl on the planet, okay?" Dawn said. "But I'd really, really appreciate it if you didn't treat me that way."

And then my dream girl swept away. And I realized something. Maybe I was the dumb one.

I should have realized that even knockouts who can't break a C don't like to feel dumb.

But before I became a total sensitive guy and was able to tune in to Dawn's feelings, I decided to spy on her Friday night.

5//watching

On Friday, my dad was going to be late, as usual, and my mom was heading out to a dinner party alone. My dad said he'd try to show up and meet her at some point. My father is a fabulously successful attorney with a thriving practice defending the just and the innocent.

He's an expensive lawyer who works very hard to get scum with money off the hook.

Probably one of my dad's major career disappointments was missing out on defending one of the football players at Bloomfield. He was trying a big case in California, and even though he called and faxed and even flew back here a few times, Jamie and the guys had already hired attorneys. My dad still can't talk about it without getting very red in the face.

My point is that my dinner hour is basically whenever I felt like popping the frozen pizza into the microwave. Which meant I could take off that evening whenever I felt like it.

Of course, I can always take off whenever I feel like it. Because basically, my parents are unaware. They lead incredibly busy lives, and as long as I get into Harvard like my brother, Steven, I'm golden.

I slid into my Volvo (Dad insisted on an ultrasafety vehicle—he also takes the occasional personal injury suit) and drove to Butler's Lake.

I parked my car in a far, dark corner of the rutted lot near the path to the lake. Dawn wasn't here yet. There was only a rusted-out Ford parked in another corner. It looked abandoned.

I wished I'd brought a flashlight. The overhanging trees shadowed the path, and I kept tripping over tree roots. I was glad Dawn hadn't arrived. She would have heard my elephant-like progress through the woods. I'm not exactly Daniel Boone.

But, luckily, I slowed down before I reached the ice-skating hut, because Dawn was there, waiting right in front. Maybe there was another parking lot I didn't know about.

The hut looked like a ramshackle dump without kids horsing around, putting on their skates and taking them off, flinging wet wool socks into other kids' faces. I melted away under the trees and watched Dawn.

She was wearing a rose-colored sweater, jeans, and boots. She shivered, just like I was doing. It was colder out here than we'd imagined. She had a small flashlight and was clutching it against her chest.

I thought about stepping forward, but I waited. Dawn peered around, still nervous. After a few minutes, she opened the door of the hut and peered inside. She swept the interior with her light. Then she closed the door again.

The darkness grew until I could just make out the white blur of her face. I could feel her nervousness across the space between us. She switched on her light again.

After a few minutes, the light flickered. Dawn shook it. It went out.

Fifteen minutes crawled by. Twenty. She was agitated now, and heading toward being scared. I could see it, could feel it. My eyes had adjusted to the darkness. It was like I was a wolf, waiting in the dark with all the time in the world to pounce.

Something about her fear made me feel powerful. She didn't know I was watching her. She didn't know someone was there, able to protect her. She thought she was alone.

I started out of the woods toward her, and she let out a small shriek. Then she recognized me.

"Brian! What are you doing here?"

I came closer through the darkness. "What do you think?"

"Well, I'm glad it's you," Dawn told me. Her blond hair shimmered in the faint light.

I stopped. "You are?"

She gazed around, still hugging herself. "Obviously, LoneLobo isn't going to show up. And this place is giving me major heebie-jeebies. Let's get out of here."

We started down the path. We had to walk slowly. Dawn slipped her arm through mine to keep her steady. Her boots had heels.

"Hey, I have an idea," I said, as if I'd just thought of it. "Let's go grab some pizza and come up with a new plan to flush out Lobo."

"I have to get to the game," Dawn said.

"But that doesn't start for over an hour," I said. "You have to eat."

"My mom left me something at home." Dawn almost tripped over a root, and held on to my arm. She nearly took me down with her, but we found our balance. "I think I'll write him again. I can use your comput-er. Maybe he just needs to be coaxed."

"Maybe he doesn't *want* to meet you," I suggested. "Aren't you mad that he made you wait out here in the cold?"

"I think he's just scared," Dawn replied. "Deep down, he's really sensitive."

Disgusted, I let Dawn's arm fall as we reached the parking lot. What was it with girls? As long as a guy is cool, they make up qualities that aren't even there. A guy can spend most of his life snapping his wet towel at everybody in the locker room, but girls will breathe words about him like "sensitive."

"That's your car?" I blurted when Dawn headed toward the beat-up Ford Falcon. Maybe I could take a lesson in sensitivity, too.

"It's my dad's. I wracked up my Jaguar last year, and they won't buy me another car until graduation. My dad says this is a classic," Dawn said, grimacing. "He's restoring it . . . slowly. Thinks it's more fun to drive than his Mercedes. Can you believe it?" She swung the door open and got inside. "Well, thanks—"

"Are you sure about that pizza?" I asked quickly. "My treat."

Dawn started the engine. "I really have to go. Thanks, Bri."

I gave her a totally phony cheerful wave. I ate her dust as she peeled out of the parking lot.

Mal was right. Girls like Dawn never look at guys like us. We're not *boyfriend material*. We're too nice. We do people favors. We study. We obey the rules.

Why do girls like Dawn always check the cool factor before falling for a guy? Why can't they look past clothes and attitude, straight into your heart?

Dawn could totally impose on me for favors, but she wouldn't be seen sharing a pizza with me.

Maybe I should teach her a lesson. For her own good. And it would teach a lesson to her friend Steffi, too. And Talia Wilson, and Debbi Genelli, and all the other perfect girls at perfect Bloomfield High.

Maybe Dawn would see that she wasn't looking at things the right way. She'd see that there was more to Brian Rittenhouse than his puny frame and his glasses.

I could strike a blow for the Brians of the world if I showed Dawn that cool wasn't everything.

6//table turning

Subj: *Aggressive Grrrlz*
Date: *Monday*
From: *LoneLobo*

Here's wassup this week: Lobo has noticed that certain upperclassgrrlz are watching a little too much Warrior Princess TV. Work it, girl, U Bet, and by the way, love that ferocious hair—but leave off the headlocks, willya?

Don't jump down my throat. I'm not saying we're not equals, yadda yadda. But in the real world, guys still like to ask girls out. At least let us pretend to have the upper hand. We're talking fragile male egos here. Kay?

Dawn was close to tears when she found me in the student council offices, trying to dream up slogans for my reelection campaign. I had some major repair work to accomplish with Mal. While I'd been skulking in the woods watching Dawn, Mal had been waiting for me. I'd forgotten that I was supposed to head to his house after school.

We were supposed to brainstorm new ideas for the campaign over dinner. Mal was still sore at me for forgetting.

"Do you think he meant me?" Dawn asked, waving a hard copy of Lobo's posting.

"I don't know," I said. "That wouldn't be very nice if he did."

Way to go, Lobo!

Dawn bit her lip in that way that drives me mad. "Steffi doesn't think so."

Not Steffi again!

"Why not?"

"Well, she says it's not like I asked Lobo for a *date*," Dawn said. "I just asked to meet him. That's different."

"Steffi has a point."

She is a clueless, pointless pain!

"Maybe he had a reason not to show up," Dawn said. "I heard that the coach made the football players come to the stadium early for a strategy session."

"Meaning?" I asked.

"Well, what if Lobo is Jason? He couldn't have made it out to the lake and back in time," Dawn explained. "So what do you think I should do?"

"Sit tight and wait," I said. "Maybe he'll contact you."

But Dawn wasn't listening. "Steffi says I should write him another e-mail. Which is what I need to talk to you about. Can I borrow your laptop?"

"I guess so," I said. "Do you want me to help you write it?"

"I can do it this time," Dawn said.

"Look, Dawn, I'm not sure if—"

"Thanks, Bri. You are such a major pal." Dawn tried to stuff the posting into her tote while reaching for my computer on the desk.

But her tote slipped off her shoulder, and she almost dropped the computer. We both dived for it, and her tote upended onto the floor. Luckily, I caught the computer.

"Gosh, Brian, I'm so sorry." Dawn fell to

her knees and started to shove things back into her tote. I bent down to help her. Lipstick, coins, crumpled-up tissues, bottled water, lip balm, textbooks, Midol, deodorant, makeup, pens . . . if you've ever wondered what's in a girl's purse, just think *everything*.

"I'm such an awful mess," Dawn said. Her voice sounded thick, like she was going to cry.

I could only see the crown of her head. I couldn't tell if she was crying. Maybe she was getting a cold. But she stuck things into her tote without looking. She jammed an open pen inside. I took it back out and capped it gently.

"Dawn, are you okay?"

She sniffed. "I don't know what's wrong with me." She looked up. Her eyes were red. "It's the pressure, you know? Sometimes high school is just so *hard*. Keeping up, and doing the right things, and clothes, and everything. . . ."

"I have a solution," I said. I handed her one of the crumpled-up tissues. I only hoped it was clean.

She dabbed at her eyes. "You do?"

"Be a nerd like me," I said. "That way you don't have to worry about fitting in. You don't fit in anywhere."

She smiled. "You are so incredibly sweet."

If there was ever a moment to kiss Dawn Sedaris, this was it. We stared at each other for a long moment.

Then she scrambled to her feet, yanking her tote over her shoulder and grabbing my computer off the desk. "I really have to run," she said.

"Don't tell me," I said. "You have to meet Steffi."

But she was already running out the door, leaving me kneeling on the floor. I sighed and started to get up. That's when I noticed a brightly colored object underneath the desk. I reached under and grabbed it.

Dawn's keys. They were attached to a ring, and tied on to it was a ball of all different colors of yarn. It looked homemade. Not the kind of key ring you'd expect Dawn to have. I'd have thought something expensive, like silver from Tiffany's, or leather.

I closed my fist over it. Here's how

pathetic I am—I got a charge out of holding Dawn Sedaris's stupid yarn key ring.

At lunchtime, I practically ran to the cafeteria. Now that Dawn had nabbed my laptop with my brilliant ideas stuck in hard drive, I had to come up with another way to get Mal to forgive me.

Apparently, Mal had not spent the most stellar of evenings. He doesn't have the greatest home life. Mal's mom had died when he was in eighth grade. She'd fallen off a ladder while she was hanging curtains in the carriage house she'd made into a painting studio. The place had very high ceilings, and she'd landed in the worst possible way. She'd broken her neck.

The grisly part was that Mal had found her. Mal had come home from school, grabbed an apple, then headed out back to say, "Mom, I'm home!"

Mal never talks about it. And I never ask. I went to the wake, and the funeral, and he practically lived at my house that year, but we basically watched videos and ate junk food. I had a tendency to stop when I was full, but Mal just kept eating.

Mal's mom had always seemed unhappy to me. Either that, or she was flitting around, smiling too much and asking if she could make you a sandwich. She wasn't a very good artist, either. Mal's father called the studio "the bunker" because she'd bought those heavy dark curtains for the windows. She'd said the light distracted her. I guess she should have let the sun shine in.

Anyway, what I'm trying to say is that Mal's parents weren't exactly happy together, even when Mrs. Bouchard was alive. But Mal had been really close to her. Mr. Bouchard works all the time, and Mal and his mom had done a lot of hanging out, just the two of them.

They hired someone to clean out the bunker afterward of all the painting supplies. But Mal and his dad never stepped foot inside. The garage was filled with gardening equipment and power mowers and leaf blowers and boxes, and Mal had to park in the driveway, even during a blizzard. But they still wouldn't move anything into the bunker.

Now, Mal and his dad don't talk much. And Mr. Bouchard has really slid toward the deep end of the dysfunctional pool. He is still a successful businessman. He owns this chain of audio stores and has a million investments. But he drinks too much and doesn't pay much attention to Mal. So Mal tries not to be home when his dad is around.

"Let me give you a glimpse into my evening," Mal had told me furiously when he'd finally reached me on Saturday morning. "First of all, Dad decided to cook dinner, for some reason. Only he was too soused to really do it, of course, so he ended up starting a fire in the oven. Like he knows how to cook pot roast! And Rosalia had left all this food in the fridge for the weekend, like she always does. He didn't need to cook!"

"So what happened?" I asked.

"I put out the fire with the extinguisher," Mal said. "We left the whole mess for Rosalia to clean up on Monday. Dad ate macaroni and cheese without even heating it up. Talk about gross. Then he says he's going to the club to hit golf balls. So I say,

'They let you hit golf balls at the bar now?'—and he gets pissed. He goes out, gets in the car, and backs down the driveway—right into a tree."

"Wow. Is he okay?"

"He's fine. He was just embarrassed. I brought him inside and put him to bed. He was crying. It was totally bizarre."

"Wow," I said.

"My mom died around this time," Mal said.

"Oh," I said. Now I felt like a completely horrible friend. I hadn't remembered that grim anniversary. What a time to pick to ditch Mal. Now what could I possibly say?

So I gave the heartfelt guy sympathy response.

"Man," I said.

"Yeah," Mal said, which was the appropriate reply. "Anyway, thanks for ditching me. It was a delightful evening. I'm so glad you made sure I didn't miss it."

It was time for a grand gesture. Mal was my bud. I had to make it up to him.

So on Monday I wanted to beat him to the cafeteria, and I did. I loaded my tray with blueberry muffins, pudding, cake, chocolate milk, and those awful cookies Mal wolfs down by the dozen. Then I lined them all up in front of Mal's usual place at the table.

He arrived with a full tray and stared at the array of sugar and carbs.

"And I didn't get you anything," he finally said.

He didn't even crack a smile. But I knew we were friends again.

"Okay, let's talk strategy," I said as we chowed down on our grilled ham and cheese sandwiches. "I'm ready to get serious."

"Well, Polemus is blowing us away," Mal said. "I came up with the poster design over the weekend. You can check it out after lunch. Then I was thinking about doing some cafeteria chats—visiting each table and pitching your candidacy. We could figure out exactly what kinds of things to say—"

I am ashamed to report that right about there, I tuned Mal out. I know I said I was ready to get serious. I was ready to make it up to him by concentrating on the election. But now that he'd forgiven me, I started thinking about Dawn again.

Seeing her cry that way had only made me more determined to make her see that her vision of Lobo was an illusion. She had to see *me*.

I remembered that powerful feeling of wanting to protect her. I remembered how glad she'd been to see me at the pond.

Maybe that was the way to go. If I could really make her scared of the danger of falling in love with a fantasy, she would naturally look to me for protection. And I wouldn't be lying, exactly. Principal Bigelow had warned me that the police thought there was another murderer on the loose. What if there really was?

Mal blabbed on, and ate most of the junk food. The bell rang, and I headed to my next class. I look forward to English all day, because Dawn is in my class. Of course, I sit in the front, and she sits over by the windows with Debbi Genelli and Troy Sanderson and all the other Chosen Ones.

I waved at Dawn across the room, but

she didn't see me. She was laughing at something Troy had said. It was hard to remember the teary Dawn who had told me how hard high school was.

I reached into my backpack to get out my notebook and pen. My hand closed over the fluffy key ring. I was about to hold it up and wave it at Dawn, but I stopped. I left my hand closed over it.

Because I suddenly knew what my next step would be. It would make me cross that line from Nice Guy to Stinker.

But I didn't care.

7//one step over the line

You may or may not know this, but in order to defend the worst lowlifes in the country, you need a snappy wardrobe. When my dad isn't charging huge retainers, he's on the phone to his tailor in Chicago.

He's a fanatic about organization, too. He has a huge walk-in closet, and everything is coordinated by color. He has gray, navy, and black suits, and the particular tie for each suit hangs on a special hanger right next to it. He even pins coordinating socks to his suits. What I'm leading up to is that my dad is just the type of guy to have an old-fashioned shoe-shine kit.

I took it from his closet and removed a jar of black shoe polish. Then I went to work on Dawn's key ring. Soon, I'd dyed it completely black.

I replaced Dad's kit at the proper angle on his closet shelf. Then I printed a note out on my computer:

SOMEDAY YOU WILL DIE.

I wrapped the note around the key ring and sealed it with tape. The next step was getting it into Dawn's hands.

There, I had a slight problem. She wasn't in the phone book. She wasn't listed on the Internet.

Last year, Mal had hacked his way into the records of the nurse's office at school. It was an easy way to get every student's address. He'd made some sort of macro program and sent this campaign brochure to everyone's house.

But I'm no hacker. And I couldn't exactly ask Mal.

There was only one thing left to do. Sneak it back into her tote bag.

The next day at school, I waited and watched for the best time to make my move. I discovered that Dawn is easily distracted. She is always leaving her bag lying over a chair, or dumping it on the floor in order to have her hands free for conversation. Occasionally, she trips over it. I realized that my dream girl is something of a klutz.

Naturally, I only worshiped her more.

Finally, I seized my moment. Dawn set her bag down on the floor in order to work her locker combination. She was holding a can of diet soda in one hand and trying to twirl the lock at the same time. She spilled the soda on her shirt just as the locker door popped open. She quickly grabbed a T-shirt from her locker and began to dab at it.

I came up from behind, slipped the paper-wrapped key ring into her tote bag, and popped around the door, asking, "Anything I can do?"

I got points for coming up with a bunch of tissues to wipe up the stain. And I achieved my mission.

Totally ferocious, or what?

The next day, the news raced through the halls. The 24 Point Club was back! Dawn had told Steffi Minor, who most likely had burned out several batteries on her cell phone telling people the news.

Rumor had it that Dawn Sedaris was terrified. She was going to stay home from school, but then she decided she'd be more afraid at home. Debbi Genelli had advised her to talk to her parents about getting a deluxe system from her dad's company, Genelli Security.

I kept looking for Dawn, but I didn't even catch a glimpse. I knew I'd see her in the cafeteria, or later, in English class, so I didn't sweat it too much. Besides, I was a little nervous that Dawn might connect losing her keys to that day in the student council office.

As usual, Mal took the news badly.

"This is a disaster for us," he told me outside his calculus class. "I've put up all those Move On with Brian—Get the Pride Back posters already. Now we're going to look like idiots."

"I bet it all dies down in a day or so," I said.

Mal looked mournful. "Are you kidding? That Detective Hanigan is here again, stirring the pot. And the pot's already boiling, bud. It's red hot!"

I got a jolt when Mal mentioned the police. Somehow, I hadn't factored them into the equation. I hadn't expected the whole school to find out about Dawn's key ring. Somehow, I imagined her coming to me, saying, *Oh, Brian. You're so smart. What should I do?*

Instead, she'd told Steffi. She might as well have announced it on the evening news. "Hanigan has already interviewed Dawn and Steffi," Mal said with a sigh. "It's only a matter of time before the reporters show up. This is not going to go away."

So maybe I hadn't thought things through. Maybe I'd gone just a tad over the line. But wasn't Dawn worth it?

I didn't see Dawn in the cafeteria at lunch, or in English later. But I finally caught up to her before last period. I was heading to class when I passed the empty chem lab. To my surprise, Dawn was sitting at one of the tables, staring into space.

"Hi," I said, walking in. "The bell rang, you know. It's time for class."

"Yeah," Dawn said.

"Are you coming?"

"I don't know," Dawn whispered.

I closed the door behind me and drew up a stool next to her. "Tell me about it," I said.

Her face looked pale. Her hair was scraped back in a ponytail. If she'd started out the day with lip gloss, it had all been chewed off. But she still looked so pretty.

"It's so weird, Brian. It's like, I can't walk through the halls, or eat lunch, or go to class. I look around and wonder, *Who is it?* Who sent me that . . . thing?" She shivered. "And the police detective told me that it looks like there really is a murderer still here at Bloomfield High. And he's targeted *me!*" Her voice grew shrill. "Why? Why me? Do you think it's a warning?"

"A warning about what?" I asked, puzzled.

"It's no secret that Hanigan was going to interview me," Dawn said. "What if the ringleader guy was trying to scare me off?"

"But you don't know anything," I said reassuringly.

She grabbed my arm. "But he doesn't know that!"

"Dawn, calm down," I said. "It was probably a prank. The trial is coming up. Some stupid jerk with a bad sense of humor is yanking your chain. If someone really wanted to scare you, wouldn't he have sent you a warning before you talked to Hanigan? Look, you and I both know that Bloomfield is full of jerks with bad senses of humor. I'm sure you've even dated a couple."

She let out a soft laugh. Then she sort of collapsed on my shoulder. The impact of her scent and the feel of her hair almost sent me crashing to the floor. Luckily, I remembered to be manly and stay upright.

"Do you really think that?" she asked.

"I do," I said firmly.

Dawn's voice was muffled. "I want to think that. But I look at everyone, and I wonder. I never even sent another e-mail to Lobo. I don't even trust *him* anymore. I don't trust anyone."

She drew away. Her eyes looked so blue in her pale face. They're this totally unique color, like a lake in the early morning. Dark, shadowy blue.

"Except you, Brian," she whispered.

"Sometimes I wonder if you're my only friend."

And at that moment, I realized that I'd done exactly the right thing.

8//everybody wants lobo

Subj: *Been There, Done That, Got the T-Shirt*
Date: *Thursday*
From: *LoneLobo*

Lobo thinks it's way past time to yell CHILL at the gloom and doom-fuls who think just because a certain senior got her key chain rolled in mud that it means the 24 Pt Club is back.

Relax, everybody. It's not a murderer. It's just someone with a really bad sense of humor. Let's face it—when it comes to the senior class, we could all wear an "I'm with Stupid" T-shirt.

So get over yourselves. And while you do, everybody—I keep saying this—grow up, willya?

* * *

"Lobo is right," Steffi declared. She tucked her short dark hair behind her ears and leaned across the table. She pointed a finger at Dawn. "Get over yourself."

"It's not that easy," Dawn said. She took a sip of soda.

I was in a privileged position. I was actually at the cafeteria table of two members of the Chosen Few. Dawn had been waiting outside my social studies class.

"Will you have lunch with me?" she'd asked.

I shrugged. "Sure."

What she didn't know was, she could have said, *Will you wash my gym uniform?* or, *Will you clip my toenails?* and I would have agreed.

"Well, I have a piece of information that should change your mind *real* fast," Steffi said. She looked around the cafeteria, then leaned over in order to whisper.

What a phony. As if she wouldn't be sharing all details of this conversation next period with Debbi or Tiffany or Talia, or whomever else would listen.

"I have news about your ex," she said.

Dawn looked up from her soda. "Mark?"

I didn't like the way she looked up. I didn't like the way she said his name.

"He asked me a million questions about you," Steffi told her in a low voice. "About how you were doing, if you were still scared, if the police were taking the threat seriously, all that. He's really concerned, Dawn."

"Really?" Dawn said.

I didn't like the way she asked it.

"And do you know what else? He said that everybody was just making it worse for you by taking the whole thing seriously. He said they were just a bunch of doom-mongers. *Doom-mongers,* Dawn! Get it? That's what Lobo said!"

"Actually, he said doom-*fuls,*" I pointed out.

But Dawn and Steffi weren't paying attention to me. They were staring at each other, openmouthed.

"You think?" Dawn breathed.

Steffi nodded sagely. "I think. Def-in-ite-ly," she said, pronouncing each syllable.

"Wow," Dawn said. "Mark."

I hated the way she said his name. Steffi just kept nodding at her, like one of those tacky statues in the rear window of a car.

Steffi Minor is, by her own description, "a people person." Every high school needs someone like Steffi to throw parties, give people zany nicknames, and volunteer on dance committees. I myself, as student council president, had often been grateful for her help and support.

She was toast.

"Hey, wait up!"

Someone was yelling behind me, but I didn't turn. Whenever anyone yelled at someone to "wait up," they were never yelling at me.

I had banged out of school as soon as the bell rang. I was in a totally foul mood, and I was ditching Chess Club. Chess is a fascinating, compelling game of strategy and is considered excellent training for the analytical mind.

I thought it would look good on my transcripts. Hello, Harvard!

"Excuse me? Excuse me?"

I turned around. A slightly overweight, middle-aged woman wearing one of those barn jackets with about a thousand pockets was barreling down the path toward me. She had short red hair that was a mass of curls, and her blouse was halfway out of her skirt. She was carrying the biggest paper cup of coffee I'd ever seen.

"Brian Rittenhouse, right?" she asked.

I nodded. "Can I help you?" It was my polite-to-adults voice. I couldn't imagine who this woman was. Maybe a recently divorced housewife who'd gone back to college to finish up her teaching degree and was sitting in on classes. Or the mother of someone like weird Ursula Malinger, a definite Void, whose skin once turned orange because all she ate was carrots. Or—

"I'm Detective Hanigan," she said.

Well, *gulp*.

I must have looked surprised, because she sipped her coffee and grinned at me. "Yeah, I really am. Got a minute?"

And I'd almost made the parking lot. "I was just about to head home," I said. Then

I realized that I should be extremely cooper-ative. "But yeah, sure."

She hitched her purse higher on her shoulder and took another gulp of coffee. "I'll walk you to your car."

We struck off down the path toward the parking lot together. She was wearing green suede loafers with thick rubber soles. The suede was spotted, as though she'd been caught in a rainstorm. She had a lot to learn about how to treat suede. Maybe Hanigan should be talking to my dad.

"Principal Bigelow says you're the guy to talk to about things around here," she said. Her eyes were the color of caramels. Soft and golden. Not the eyes of a crackerjack detective. I started to relax a little bit. Detective Sloppy was no match for me.

"I don't know about that," I said mod-estly. "But I'll try to help."

"You know that a dyed key ring was sent to Dawn Sedaris," Detective Hanigan said.

I nodded. "It's all over the school."

She took a sip of coffee as we walked. Some of it spilled on her shirt, and she rubbed it in. "So what do you think about it?"

I frowned, pretending to think. "I don't know. Some people are saying that it's a copycat thing. A practical joke."

"Is that what you think?"

I shrugged again. "Maybe. Kids can be pretty cruel. Maybe whoever did it had a grudge against Dawn."

"Why would someone have a grudge against Dawn?"

Oops. Detective Hanigan's tone had sharpened. "No reason," I said. "She's really popular."

"Lots of dates? Boyfriends?"

"Sure," I said. "She dated Mark Skeeter last year. They had a pretty bad breakup."

"Mark Skeeter," Detective Hanigan repeated, nodding.

"He's the editor of the *Scroll*. The school paper." I tried to look anxious. "Not that I'm saying he did anything. Gosh."

"No, no, of course not. Hey, nice car." We'd stopped by my car, and Hanigan patted it. "I'd like to get a Volvo. They're real safe."

"What do you drive?" I asked politely.

"A Ferrari," Hanigan said.

She grinned at my stunned expression. "Relax. Just kidding, Brian. So do you know who Lobo is?"

"Lobo?" I stopped fishing for my keys. "No, of course not. Nobody does."

"Is there any way to find out who he is?"

"Like how?" I asked.

She shrugged while she swirled her coffee. "You have to know who some of the names on the message board belong to. Right?"

"Well, yes. Some names are obvious—everyone knows that Kimbo is Kimberly Jones, and CMinus is Chris Wilder, for example. My posting name is prez.bri. But there are at least three or four names that are anonymous, just like Lobo."

"Mmmm. Now, what did I want to ask you . . . shoot. I completely lost my train of thought." She took a gulp of coffee. "Oh. Could you get me a hard copy of the message board postings?"

I nodded. "It only goes back about two weeks, though. Then it's erased."

"That's okay. Have you ever thought about who Lobo might be? Is he a jock?"

"I don't know how I'd know that," I said.

"From things he says," Hanigan said, shrugging. "Like, for example, if he talks about the football games, does it seem like he really *knows?*"

I pretended to think. "Hmmm. I don't know. I'd have to think about it. I mean, I never noticed it in the past. I guess I wasn't very interested."

"But you post regularly," Hanigan said. She smiled. "So I'm told. You must be a little curious."

"Not really," I said. "I like the fact that the postings are anonymous. That's the fun of it."

"Then why didn't you pick a more anonymous online name?" Hanigan asked pleasantly. "'Prez.bri' is fairly obvious."

Maybe Detective Sloppy wasn't as clueless as I'd thought.

"What I mean is, for me, the postings are like a sounding board," I said. "I get to know what the students are really thinking. It's really helpful."

"Ah. You're a real politician, I see."

Hanigan drained her coffee. She looked around for a wastebasket, but there wasn't one. "Well, I'm going to take off. . . . Oh, wait. Was Lobo on the board last year? Around the time of the Coach Cappistrano murder?"

I nodded. "We started the Water Fountain last fall. It took a while to catch on, but yeah, I think Lobo was posting from the beginning." I hesitated. "Detective Hanigan, are you saying that Lobo might have been in the 24 Point Club?"

"I don't think I said that, Brian," Hanigan answered. She crumpled up her coffee cup. Some liquid escaped, and a few drops fell on her suede shoe. "But as long as we're on the subject, how do you know he's not?"

I jingled my car keys. "I don't. But—"

"Nice talking to you, Brian," Detective Hanigan said smoothly. "I'll get back to you about that hard copy."

And she walked away, leaving a trail of coffee drops behind her.

* * *

"If this is the best the police department

can come up with, Coach Cappistrano will never rest in peace," I told Mal later that afternoon.

I'd gone over to look at his campaign idea—a fake mock-up of a sample front page of the *Scroll* with a headline announcing that I was the best candidate. We'd done the same thing last year, and it had been a huge hit. Mal thought that kids would get a kick out of seeing it again.

Mal had even put in proofreading symbols and typesetting directions, as though the paper was about to go to press. It looked totally authentic.

Every article on the front page was also about me. I had to admit I liked the look of it. After I'd approved the design, we headed to the kitchen so that Mal could have— guess what?—a snack.

"When she isn't spilling coffee, she's trying to remember what she wanted to ask," I said. "If you ask me, Detective Sloppy is going to get exactly nowhere."

Mal cracked an egg and dumped it in a paper cup. Then he unwrapped a slice of American cheese and shredded it in the mixture. He added a dollop of Tabasco sauce, then popped it into the microwave. "Want one?"

"Gee, it looks totally gourmet," I said. "But no thanks."

"You know, you really surprise me, bud," Mal said, leaning against the counter. "Aren't you part of the media-mad generation? Aren't you an accomplished channel-surfer?"

"Yeah, so?" I said.

The microwave dinged, and Mal began to scoop out this goopy eggy-cheesy mixture from the cup. "So, haven't you ever seen *Columbo*? The detective with the wrinkly raincoat who always forgets what he came to ask? Sounds like your Detective Sloppy has watched plenty of TV. And may I point out that Columbo always solves his cases?"

I snorted. "That still doesn't mean she's a hotshot detective."

"Sounds like she's lined up Lobo in her sights to me," Mal said, scooping up the last of the goop. "I wonder if there's any ice cream left?"

He loped over to the freezer and rooted through it. He came out with a carton of fudge ripple. He dug into it with his eggy spoon.

"If you think about it, it makes total sense," Mal said around a mouthful of ice cream. "The head of the 24 Point Club would have to be a leader. A totally cool guy that the intellectually challenged football players would look up to. Somebody with nerve and brains. She might be on the right track." He waved the spoon at me. "I'll tell you something, bud. If I were Lobo, I'd be worried—whether I was the ringleader or not."

I pretended to be skeptical, but what Mal had said registered, big time. He is stone-cold brilliant. He doesn't get the best grades, but that's because he barely cracks a book. His test scores are in the stratosphere. I totally trust his instincts. If he thought Lobo was in trouble, Lobo was in trouble.

"Do you have any idea who he is?" Mal asked me. "I mean, just between us? You've been trying to scope him out for Dawn."

"Not a clue," I said.

I don't lie to Mal very often. But occasionally, an untruth is called for.

Because I am Lobo.

9//accessing lobo

Hope I didn't shock you. But did you ever study the concept of the "unreliable narrator" in English class? You can't trust everything you read.

Okay, let me ask you this. If you're basically a nice, good person who says reasonable things and tries not to hurt people, well—goody for you.

But haven't you ever been tempted to tell people what you *really* think?

Sure you have.

Here's my problem. Since day one, freshman year, I've either been running for office or representing my school. I always have to watch what I say. I have to be polite. I have to support school policies. I have to applaud every school activity—from football to Future Farmers of America.

That can take a toll on a guy.

When the Water Fountain started in the fall of my junior year, I didn't think much of it. I logged on as prez.bri and did my usual gig, talking about how the teachers need our support and school loyalty is our first priority and the Wolverines are going all the way this year.

Rah rah blah.

Then the Players, the drama club, put on the worst revue you've ever seen. I'd been around for rehearsals, so I knew the real story. The head of the club, Mrs. Titano, had a slight revolution on her hands. All the kids who never got parts were threatening to quit. The fact that they were without a speck of talent hadn't occurred to them. So Mrs. Titano was in a tight spot. If there weren't enough kids in the club, it would be dissolved. And that wouldn't look good. So she let all the kids who complained into this "open revue."

You've never seen anything so awful in your life. She tried to sprinkle in some good stuff—Dawn did a reading, which was stellar, of course, and Andy Maloney played the guitar—but there was only so much she could do.

As prez.bri, I had to support the school. Not to mention that Mal has drummed into my head that *every student is a vote!* I wanted to trash the thing. Big time.

I gave it a rave.

But it didn't feel right. So I had an inspiration. I made up another online address— LoneLobo—and logged on. I gave the review I really wanted to give. I trashed DeDee Ballard's hip-hop dance. I made fun of Alex Quigley's trumpet playing. And when I got to Cindie Bonner singing an old Neil Young song, the gloves were off. I think I said something about "a mouse on Prozac."

I'd never felt so good in my life.

Then I watched the reactions pile in. Kids were either outraged at how mean I was, or thought I was hysterical. So I reacted to the reactions, and Lobo got a rep.

I haven't looked back since. Every time there's an issue at school, or a hot piece of gossip, Lobo weighs in. On Mondays, everyone tunes in to the Water Fountain to see what topic Lobo will bring up that week. I think even teachers snoop, even though it's supposed to be kids only.

Meanwhile, safe, polite Brian Rittenhouse drones on about school spirit. Sometimes, I even have Brian argue with Lobo, just in case someone starts to wonder if I could be him.

But who would ever figure out that nerdy Brian could be such a star? Certainly not Dawn.

It hadn't bothered me before. I liked that Lobo was a secret only I knew. I figured that Lobo was just one small part of myself.

But now, I was starting to wonder.

If Lobo was smarter about life and way cooler than me, did that mean that I was cooler than I thought? What makes someone cool, anyway? Do clothes and hair really have that much to do with it? Or do people just think they did?

And why should Brian put up with something that Lobo wouldn't? We are the same person!

So, if Steffi Minor got on Lobo's nerves, he'd find a way to neutralize her, wouldn't he? He'd blast her on the message board. He'd grind her into dust.

I'd just have to do what Lobo would do.

Because I needed to be the only one whom Dawn would trust.

She has to finish her column every Monday by the end of lunch. She doesn't want to stay any later at school than she has to.

I remembered Dawn's words, and I had a way to get Steffi off my back.

On Monday, I hung around after school. There weren't that many club meetings on Mondays, so the school felt empty. I stayed in the student council office, pretending to use the computer.

Slowly, I heard the school shut down around me. I knew there was swimming practice, but the pool was in the new wing, on the lower level.

I waited until four-thirty. Then I eased out into the hall. Completely empty.

What is it about an empty school that makes you want to do bad things?

My heart was slamming against my chest, and I hadn't even done anything yet. I headed down one flight to the *Scroll* office. Empty. I'd been worried that Mark and Emily would still be working.

Mark's desk was the one with the sign behind it that read BIG CHEESE DEADLINE CRUNCHER. Emily is "Cheese Jr." I turned on her computer and searched her files. It was child's play to find Steffi's column for Wednesday's paper. There was a code attached that said that it had already been proofed. Good.

It was even easier to imitate Steffi's gushy prose.

Listen up, kiddies. What morning star has developed a major jones for our anonymous wolf? She enlisted the aid of our commander in chief, even arranged a meeting with the guy, but he didn't show. Boo-hoo! Poor baby! Forbidden love is the worst. Just ask Juliet.

But our rosy morning star has another prob. Namely, her ex. He keeps buzzing around, she keeps swatting—but he just won't take the hint. Need a can of Raid, hon? Just tell him you run with the wolves—not the insects.

As long as I was at it, I might as well get rid of Mark Skeeter, too. His nickname is Mosquito, although he isn't crazy about you calling him that to his face.

I clicked on "send to layout."

Now all I had to do was sit back and watch the fur fly.

I sat there, chuckling. In the silence, it sounded close to maniacal. But I'd never felt so in control in my life.

The Scroll comes out each Wednesday morning. Dave Mackenzie, the managing editor, usually drops a big stack on the front steps so that everyone can pick it up before school starts. The first thing kids usually read is Steffi's column.

My vantage point was by the bike rack. I had a perfect view of the Chosen Few. Dawn arrived and picked up her paper, then sauntered over to Debbi and Talia. They had already read the column, so they greeted Dawn with amused glances and secret smiles. I could see Dawn's faint puzzlement. Why were they smirking at each other that way?

Read the paper, doll, I told her silently.

Come on. That's it. Open it up. Turn to page three. Read.

I saw Dawn's face change color. Steffi is her best friend. The fact that she'd broadcast Dawn's crush for everyone to read was a major betrayal.

Away from the Cool Ones, Mark Skeeter stood leaning against the tree. He flipped through the paper, checking headlines and photos, reading some articles.

Turn to page three, Mosquito. Scan it.

I saw Mark's face turn red. He glanced over at Dawn. She didn't notice. She was staring ahead toward the parking lot.

Steffi swung down the walk, her dark hair gleaming, her miniskirt swinging, heading right for disaster. She waved at Dawn. Dawn didn't wave back.

"How's every little thing?" she called.

Steffi approached Dawn, who bent closer and spit out some words really fast. I wished I could hear. Steffi tried to protest, but Dawn just shook her head and ran off. She almost slammed into Mark. Dawn tried to talk to him, but Mark ignored her. He pushed past her and hurried into school.

Oh, what a beautiful morning.

Steffi looked as though she'd been clocked by a baseball bat. She picked up the paper that Dawn had dropped on the lawn. She scanned her column. She read it slowly. I knew I should walk away, but I couldn't stop watching.

Then she looked over the top of the paper, right at me.

She stalked toward me. I didn't move.

"Steffi!" I said. "How's every little thing?"

"You're the only one who could have done this, Brian Rittenhouse," she spat out. "Don't think I don't know it."

"Know what?"

She poked my chest. "And I know you have a major crush on Dawn. You are delusional. She'll never look twice at a scrawny loser like you. And she'll figure out that you did it."

I couldn't resist smiling at her. "She'll never believe I'd hurt her that way, Steffi. But you hurt people that way all the time, don't you. You're the gossip columnist."

"I'm a journalist!" she screeched.

"You're a hack," I said. "Mark won't even proofread your column, it stinks so bad. He makes Emily do it."

All the blood drained from her face. Even her lips looked white. They were trembling. I was fascinated. I'd never seen someone so angry before.

"I'll get you for this, Brian," she said in a choked voice. "I'll fight your election, all the way. You're nobody! You're nothing!"

She ran off. Her words hadn't even penetrated. She'd meant them as arrows, but they'd been like the wings of a butterfly against my skin.

She couldn't hurt me. She couldn't hurt Lobo, We were more powerful than she could ever imagine.

"What did you do to Steffi Minor, man?" Mal asked me the next day. He shook his head. "She's trashing your candidacy all over school."

"Who listens to what Steffi thinks about student government?" I scoffed. "If you want the scoop on who's dating who behind whose back, sure, you go to Steffi. She's just a minor inconvenience." I chortled and nudged Mal with my elbow. "A *minor* inconvenience. Get it?"

"I got it," Mal said tiredly. "She's an opinion swinger, bud. She was always on your side before. But she's not your worst problem."

"What's my worst problem?" I asked. I wasn't worried. Whatever it was, Lobo could handle it.

"I've done a straw poll," Mal told me, leaning against the locker next to mine. "Just an informal type thing. I e-mailed ballots to a random portion of the senior class. You got two votes, and Jason Polemus got all the rest. It doesn't look good."

"He's really winning?" I asked, surprised.

"What have I been telling you for the past two weeks?" Mal complained. "The election is next week. You have to get focused. I can't do all the work."

"Okay, I'll work the cafeteria at lunch," I told Mal. "I've got the experience. The accomplishments. I just need to remind everybody of that."

Mal shook his head. "You're not getting

it. You don't have the one thing Jason has. And if you have that one thing, you don't need anything else."

"A girlfriend?" I asked. Jason had recently started dating the extremely babe-a-licious Heather DeStacy.

"Charisma," Mal said sadly. "Jason's got it."

"Mal, don't look so gloom and doomful," I said. "We'll pull it off. We always do."

"Listen to me, bud," Mal said in a low, urgent voice. "This is *senior year*. It's what we've been working for. Imagine not being a member of the powerati anymore. Nobody will ask you for a favor. None of the Chosen Few will lobby you to try to get a Senior Half Day, or extend their off-campus privileges. Do you still think you'll be invited to Debbi Genelli's annual bash if you're not the president? Will Dawn Sedaris come to you for favors?"

Mal shook his head. "You'll be just Brian Rittenhouse, class nerd, living on Planet Nowheresville again. You'll be a *Void,* man. Think about it."

Mal took off, loping down the hall, his head sunk forward even more than usual.

He'd meant to scare me, and he had. I couldn't lose what I had worked so hard for. But I no longer had time to shake hands, chat people up, make speeches.

There was a better way. Lobo's way.

10//no big deal

Here's the thing. Charisma is unstable. It rises and falls on something as elusive as attitude. As fragile as the heart. As simple as fear.

I knew the format for in-school administrative memos. Mrs. Beebe sends one to all student council officers, announcing changes in school policy, or upcoming events or meetings.

First, I composed an e-mail memo on my own computer.

To: *Principal Bigelow*
From: *Ass't. Principal Beebe*
Re: *Coach Cappistrano's
           Personal Effects*

Maintenance has informed me that the locker that still contains some of Coach

Cappistrano's personal items is needed by gym staff. These items include clothing, books, toiletries, and personal papers.

Since Coach Cappistrano left no family, I'm not sure how to dispose of the above. It doesn't seem right to throw some of it away.

I'm particularly concerned about some personal papers that we wouldn't want to go public, considering the recent scandal. Not to mention the student's right to privacy. I'm referring, of course, to Jason Polemus's steroid use last year. Cappy had several memos pertaining to it, and how worried he was about Jason. I suggest we destroy them. Please advise.

What can I say? Charisma is a fragile thing.

I drove home after school, as usual. But I drove back around five o'clock. The doors were still open. I knew that there were try-outs for the first Players production of the season, *The Unsinkable Molly Brown.* Those usually ran pretty late. But the theater was in the new wing, and administrative offices were in the old.

Principal Bigelow and Mrs. Beebe were

long gone. The doors to the office were open, probably for the cleaning staff. I'd better be quick.

I turned on Mrs. Beebe's computer. I accessed the word processing software program and found her "memos" file. I slipped my disk into her computer and saved the memo I'd composed onto her hard drive.

Then, I accessed a macro that would send the memo to each member of the administrative staff. I added a list of all the student council officers.

Bingo.

Mrs. Beebe is notorious at school for her scattered ways. Bigelow doesn't fire her because (a) he's just as clueless; and (b) her husband is on disability and she needs the work. Everyone would totally believe that she made a stupid mistake.

I sent the memo to the printer. It came out crisp and clear on Bloomfield High stationery.

Then I tiptoed next door and slipped the memo into everyone's mailbox. I came out one short, so I had to run back and print another copy. That was my only nervous moment. It would be awful to come so close and then get caught.

But I didn't get caught. I slipped out as quietly as I'd slipped in. Then I headed for the nearest exit.

"Brian! What are you doing here?"

Drat. It was Mal. He was putting up a poster on the wall. A poster about me. It was the mock-up of the front page of the *Scroll*.

THE BEST MAN WINS! BRIAN RITTENHOUSE BY A LANDSLIDE!

"Tryouts for the musical," I said.

Mal laughed. "You can't sing a note."

"Yeah, but I thought it might be good to offer support." I may not be an actor, but I know how to improvise. "Maybe I could swing a few votes."

"So what are you doing in the old wing?" Mal asked.

He wasn't suspicious. He was just puzzled.

More improv!

"Nature calls," I said, gesturing at the bathroom. "And the janitor just rendered the one across from the auditorium unusable."

"If you ask me, there are better ways to get votes than to watch a bunch of girls singing off-key," Mal said as he tacked the poster to the wall. "But what do I know?"

"Relax, Mal, old bud," I said. "I have it all under control."

I have to admit that I liked myself a lot on the drive home. By this time next week, I would be Prez Bri once more.

So maybe you're thinking that I didn't play fair. And maybe I didn't. But let me ask you this. Didn't I deserve to be president again? Hadn't I slaved for three years? Hadn't I been to endless boring meetings? Hadn't I instituted the Electronic Suggestion Box and read every single entry?

What had Jason Polemus done besides throw a leather ball?

I was chuckling as I opened my front door. I stopped in the hall, hearing voices from the living room. My dad was home, which was my first major surprise. It was only five-thirty. Dad had shown up for dinner. Strike up the band.

I got a second surprise when I walked

into the living room. Detective Hanigan was sipping coffee and talking to my parents.

The air seemed to compress around me. My ears felt fuzzy. My fingertips tingled. My head felt very large, like an overinflated balloon. That's what guilt will do to you.

"Brian, hi," Detective Hanigan said. "I came by for that hard copy of the Water Fountain."

My body deflated. Anxiety rushed out of me like a fast tide. I thought I might live. Hanigan didn't suspect me.

"I'm real sorry, Detective Hanigan," I said. "It completely slipped my mind. But I promise I'll do it tomorrow. Can I e-mail it to you?"

"Sure. Let me find my card." Detective Hanigan started to rummage through her leather purse, which was on my mother's Persian rug. "Hey, nice rug."

"Thank you," my mom said. Her ankles were crossed in her lady-of-the-house mode. "Would you care for more coffee, Detective?"

"Jeez. I would, but I've got to run." Detective Hanigan finally fished out a card.

I crossed the room and took it from her hand. "Tomorrow would be great, Brian. I really appreciate this."

Detective Hanigan sipped her coffee. She looked around at the living room over the rim of her cup. My mom had hired a decorator from Chicago, so it was pretty swell. Lots of velvet and tassels and a gilt mirror over the carved wood fireplace. "The chateau look is very in," the decorator had said.

"Sure, if you're Marie Antoinette," I'd said. "And look what happened to her." But nobody paid attention. Nobody ever pays attention to me.

"This is some gorgeous room," Detective Hanigan said. "You should see my place. I still have my desk from my dorm room in college. Can you believe that?"

Nobody answered. My mother gave a strained smile. I could tell they could hardly wait for Hanigan to leave so that they could start on cocktails. Entertaining the lower classes is difficult for my mom. My dad is an old street fighter, at least.

Hanigan reached down for her purse. She

paused. Something had caught her eye. Was it the fireplace tools, or the fringe on the armchair?

"Now, just look at your gorgeous shoes," she said to my dad. "You know what I think? We've lost the art of the shoe-shine. Men just don't care anymore. My father got a shoe-shine every day of his life. In the subway, in New York. On the way up to his office. Who does that now? Nobody."

My father looked at his perfectly shod feet with satisfaction. "I do."

"I can see that, sir. I can see that," Detective Hanigan said. She picked up her purse and stood up. She slung the purse over her shoulder, nearly sending a vase crashing to the hardwood. My mother winced.

"You get a shine near your office, too?" she asked.

I broke out into an instant sweat. I suddenly saw where this was heading. *Don't say it, Dad. Don't say it—*

"Actually, I have my own shoe-shine kit," Dad said. "Maybe it's old-fashioned of me. But I like to do my own."

"I think it's very wise." Detective Hanigan looked at her own shoes. They were the same spotted green suede pair she'd had on the other day. "That's what I need." She sighed.

She didn't even look at me. She was just making small talk, the way she did. Her gaze would suddenly focus on something, and she'd get off the track. That was it. I mean, how would the police know how the key ring was dyed?

I could hear Mal's voice. *Didn't you ever hear of forensics, bud?*

But Detective Hanigan's face was friendly as she smiled at me.

"Thanks again for helping out, Brian." She turned to my mom, who'd started to rise. "I can see myself out. Thanks for the chat, folks."

She left. My mom headed immediately to the cocktail cabinet. My dad rotated his foot, pleased at the sight of the light hitting his shine.

I heard the door close softly. My heart was hammering, and my brain was full of angry bees.

Coincidence, I told myself. She saw Dad's shoe, and she thought of shoe-shines. Anybody would.

Definitely.

11//the best man wins

Subj: *ElectionGate*
Date: *Wednesday*
From: *LoneLobo*

The memo is a fake. Yeah, riiiiight. Is it just Lobo, or do Bigelow and Beebe sound just a lee-tle bit defensive?

Could it be that B&B don't want yet another Bloom High Hero to go down? Jason "Muscles" Polemus is the savior of ye olde school's rep, right? The fact that his improved gridiron performance might have been . . . um, chemically boosted could be ve-ry bad press.

Is it me, or is there a cover-up going on? Oh, well. I'm steering clear of Mr. Eau De Testosterone. You never know when those kinda guys will blow.

I was elected by an overwhelming margin. Jason Polemus stayed out of school for two days. When he returned, he looked dazed. And guilty. There's nothing like a little false gossip to make you feel that you've done something wrong.

The day the results were announced, I could barely walk down the hall without getting stopped every two seconds for congratulations. Everyone told me that they were never going to vote for Jason Polemus. I'd always had their vote. I knew they were lying. But what difference did it make? I had the power.

"It's just too bad that everyone couldn't understand that Jason had licked his problem," I told Mal modestly later that day in the cafeteria.

"Yeah," Mal said. "Especially when Lobo screamed, *Cover-up!* on the Water Fountain. And it didn't hurt when somebody photocopied the list of the symptoms of steroid abuse—like mood swings and violent behavior—and posted them all over the school."

"That was really going too far," I said.

The funny thing was, it hadn't been me. I wished I'd thought of it, though. "Some people have no shame," I said, biting into my tuna.

Mal gave me a look that, for just a split second, made me feel extremely weird. Like he knew I'd been involved somehow.

Then he reached for another chocolate milk and stuffed half a muffin in his mouth.

"Yeah," he said. Only it sounded like this: *Mmmyahh*.

I wasn't exactly convinced.

12//blood in the water

So right about then, I got a little cocky. I'd won the election. Hanigan hadn't been around in days. Dawn had rushed through a crowd of people in the hall to congratulate me. She'd kissed my cheek.

She'd kissed my cheek!

"Relax," Mal said. "She kisses her old aunt on the cheek. Her granny. Her *dog*."

"She was only millimeters away from my bottom lip," I said. "I think it's highly significant."

Mal rolled his eyes. But I didn't care. Inside, a revolution was churning. I didn't feel like a nobody anymore.

There was a voice in my head, and it was Lobo's voice. In a student council meeting, when Janie Fargate, vice president, had told us that the senior dance committee had decided on a disco theme, Brian said the presidential thing: "I think a disco theme is an awesome idea!" Lobo's voice blasted inside my head: *Think again, peanut head— it's an instant cliché.* Or I would keep a bright, interested expression on my face while Francesca Applegate droned on about the treasury, and inside, Lobo would be making buzz-saw noises: *Zzzzzzzzzz.*

It was getting kind of crowded inside my head. Integration was definitely number one on my list.

I was Lobo. I was Brian. Now I needed to be them, *together.*

I would have to tell Dawn first. She might be a little less angry if she was the first to know. After all, she'd get to scoop Steffi.

If I confessed to Dawn that I was Lobo, would she look beyond my glasses and scrawny physique and realize that I was The One?

I daydreamed the encounter in infinite variations.

Dawn is shocked, then overcome with relief and joy.

Dawn is angry, but I convince her why I couldn't tell her before, and she gently forgives me, hinting that romance is only a step away.

Dawn only smiles gently. She brushes her lips against my cheek. Then, she hits my lips. *Oh, Brian. Don't you think I knew all the time? I was waiting for you to have the courage to come forward.*

My fantasies were so perfect that I put off the reality. Like a title of one of those romance novels my mother is always reading because she can't sleep, I'd rather *Dream the Wild Dream.*

Poor Jason. In the shark-tank atmosphere of Bloomfield High, he was a goner. Blood was in the water, and the feeding frenzy had begun. Gossip swirled around him—*Okay, there was this time when the waitress got his order wrong like three times, and he practically ate the table! Well, did you notice how pumped up he looked after the season last year? Steroids, for sure*—and he just seemed to get smaller and smaller. Shoulders hunched, he quickly made his way from class to class, not meeting anyone's eyes. His posture was getting as bad as Mal's.

I really felt sorry for him, but what could I do?

The next Friday night, we played our main rival, Stonington High. Jason fumbled three times and missed two crucial passes. He was benched.

Poor guy.

During halftime, I watched Dawn jump on people's shoulders, turn cartwheels, and form a victory sign with three other cheerleaders. When it comes to jumping, the girl is incredibly talented.

Since I was president of the student body, I got to introduce all the halftime acts. As little as a year ago, I was a nervous rabbit, and fumbled more than Jason Polemus, if that's possible.

But now that I was Lobo, I didn't miss a step. My voice surged over the stadium through the sound system like a dictator. The crowd cheered, and the roar made my ears ring. I felt completely capable of invading a Third World country.

I could get used to this.

During the second half, I kept my eyes on Dawn. She stood on the sidelines with the rest of the cheerleaders. The bright stadium lights glinted off her blond hair. She looked like an angel. If angels wore little pleated red skirts and sweaters with snarling wolves on the front.

Tonight was the night. I would tell her tonight. She was in love with Lobo, wasn't she? That meant she was in love with me. It was time she realized it.

We lost the game. It was not shaping up to be a stellar season for the Wolverines. I noticed that no member of the team even looked at Jason as they headed for the locker room.

I knew that Dawn and the rest of the cheerleaders changed their clothes after the game. Usually, there was a party somewhere, or everyone headed to a designated spot—the lake, or the Crunch Café, or Debbi Genelli's house, which was a major mansion with a deluxe home entertainment package. Not to mention a great alarm system.

I was not invited. I may have been a Cool

Geek who, through hard work and persistence, now resided outside categorization, but that didn't mean I wasn't still ignored when I wasn't being pitied.

So I waited for Dawn outside the locker room. I kept in the shadows. The cheerleaders left one by one. Most of the football players headed off, too. The new coach sprinted to his Cherokee. He was probably hurrying home to update his résumé. As my father said at the only PTA meeting he'd ever attended, *Coaches at Bloomfield aren't hired to lose games!*

Just when I thought I'd have to invade the cheerleader's locker room, Dawn came out. She swung open the door, then hesitated. I took a step forward, then realized that she was waiting, holding the door open for someone behind her.

Jason Polemus appeared, hurrying a little because Dawn was holding the door. He said something to her, and she laughed.

Just don't start talking. He's a loser, Dawn! Ignore him! Brush him off, the way you brush off all the losers!

They stopped. I heard the low murmur of

their voices, but I couldn't make out the words. I heard Jason laugh this time. Dawn gestured at the parking lot. I suddenly realized what should have been apparent to me already. The rest of the cheerleaders had left. And the parking lot was empty, except for Jason's Mustang.

I could have kicked myself across the parking lot. Why hadn't I realized that? Why hadn't I come forward immediately, as soon as I'd seen her, and offered her a ride?

No! Don't leave together! Don't do it, Dawn!

They walked to Jason's Mustang. He held open the door, and she got in.

Something had to be done.

Lobo! We need to talk.

"I feel sorry for Jason," Dawn told me on Monday. I had approached her before school with the lame excuse that I needed notes from Friday's class. Like Dawn actually took good notes.

"Sorry for him?" I looked baffled. "Why?"

"Because he's being ostracized, and

there's really no evidence to convict him, you know?" Dawn shook her head, her golden hair brushing her cheeks. "Principal Bigelow and the new coach both say that Jason was never on steroids, and Mrs. Beebe says she never wrote the memo. It's this school. It's full of hypocrites. Talia is trashing Jason for having a horrible secret, and every day she throws up her lunch in the bathroom. Troy is calling him 'Chem Dude,' and he just got out of rehab. Heather broke up with him. Everyone can't wait to destroy someone. They'll tear you apart if you don't fit in."

What was Dawn worried about? She *did* fit in.

"But Lobo says the school is covering the whole thing up," I reminded her.

Dawn tossed her head. She squinted her cobalt-blue eyes. "Lobo doesn't know everything," she said. "Where does he get off, anyway?"

Huh?

"Hey, what happened to that mondo crush of yours?" I asked jovially. "You thought Lobo was the coolest."

"Well, I've changed," Dawn told me. "Or maybe Lobo has, you know? I don't like some of the things he's been saying. It was mean to accuse Jason like that." Dawn sighed. "Everything is so weird, Bri. I thought Steffi was, like, my best friend, okay? And she betrayed me. I don't know who to trust anymore."

"Lobo has been right in the past," I pointed out. "I think he's trustworthy."

Dawn looked at me curiously. "Since when are you a Lobo fan? You tried to talk me out of my crush a few weeks ago."

"But I was always a fan," I said quickly. "I think he's the hippest thing to happen to Bloomfield High since . . . since Senior Cut Day. He's cosmic."

Dawn didn't answer. She looked at me curiously. Maybe I was overselling. It was time to revert to the language of Dawn's crowd.

I shrugged. "Or whatever. Listen, Dawn, I feel sorry for Jason, too. But we have to remember the reputation of Bloomfield. Our school is all about teamwork and fair play."

I'd been playing this rah-rah song since

freshman year. I didn't even have to strain anymore, and the clichés just kept rolling out. The funny thing was, kids always swallowed them whole.

But Dawn looked past me up at the sparkling windows of Bloomfield High. The sun bounced off the gleaming surface, making the windows flash like mirrors.

"No, Brian," she said softly. "You know what Bloomfield is really about? Loneliness."

I sat in my social studies class, steaming over the fact that Dawn had eaten lunch with Jason. In my head, Lobo was sneering. *Brian, don't be a wimp. I can take care of Jason. Come on, Brian. Be a man Brian—*

At first, I thought the words in the air were in my head. Then I realized that the voice on the loudspeaker was talking to me.

"Brian Rittenhouse, please report to the principal's office immediately."

Mrs. Turkel looked over at me and nodded. I tried to assume an expression that would translate as, "Not another crisis to advise the principal on! A president's work is never done." I gathered my books and headed out.

Principal Bigelow had his serious face on when I was ushered in by a grave Mrs. Beebe. He motioned at the chair. I sat. This time, he kept the desk between us. Not a good sign.

"I'm sorry to have to tell you this, Brian," Bigelow said, folding his hands. "The student council election is now being investigated by the honor court. There were too many questions about dirty tricks. Too many rumors. Jason Polemus asked me for an investigation, and I had to agree. We have to get to the bottom of this fake memo."

I copied his serious expression and nodded. "That's probably best, sir." I kept my voice under careful control. It has a tendency to squeak under stress.

"In the meantime, of course, your presidency will have to be suspended. Janie Fargate will, as vice president, take over your duties."

Hey, Baldy, hold the phone! "Is that really necessary, sir?" I asked. "I didn't have anything to do with the memo."

"Of course not," Principal Bigelow said. "No one is suggesting that. It's just procedure. And if another election has to be called . . . well, it would be more fair to all. I had to agree with Jason and Dawn."

"Jason and *who?*" I asked. I'm afraid my voice squeaked.

"Dawn Sedaris," Principal Bigelow said. "She joined Jason in asking for an impartial investigation. She said many students are behind this."

Traitor! Did you ever hear the expression "seeing red"? Well, I saw magenta. I saw ruby. Lobo wasn't going to forget this!

"Can I ask who is heading the investigation, Mr. Bigelow?" I asked, trying to keep my voice normal.

"Emily Talladega," Bigelow said. "I'm sure she'll do a fine job."

Sure. Hand the investigation over to my major rival. No bias there.

Bigelow put on his sincere look. He leaned forward earnestly. "That memo wasn't just a mistake, Brian. It was a calculated attempt to swing the election. Now, I know you must be upset. But we have to take responsibility for our feelings. Would you like to share with me?"

I'd like to share a fist in your big red face, Cue Ball!

Shut up, Lobo!

"Brian?"

"I'm upset, I guess," I said. "But I understand."

Bigelow nodded. "Thank you for your honesty, Brian. But let's try a fresh perspective. You wouldn't want your presidency to be under a cloud, would you?"

I swallowed. "Of course not, Mr. Bigelow. I welcome any investigation, and I'll cooperate completely." I smiled broadly. "Let the sun shine in."

Lobo, come back! I need you!

13//inside looking out

Lobo knew the answer: diversion.

First, I briefed the Malmeister on what had happened in the principal's office. I drove over to his house after school to break the news.

Mal was demolishing his usual after-school snack. Today it was this special cheesecake his dad had had shipped in from Brooklyn, New York. With cherries on top.

His mouth dropped open, and it was full of cheesecake. Not a pretty sight. "This is bad," he said.

"It's not that bad," I said. "And I have this idea—"

He suddenly slammed his hand down on the table. But he missed, and it went into his piece of cheesecake.

"I'm glad to see you're taking it well," I said.

Mal lifted his hand. The sticky cherry juice ran down his forearm like blood. He looked at it sadly. "This is awful," he said. "After we worked so hard! Bigelow is an idiot. He shouldn't remove you like that."

I got up and grabbed a handful of paper towels. I handed the wad to Mal. "I think we should send out a letter to everyone in the senior class, explaining the decision and telling them that of course I'm abiding by Bigelow's decision, but I'm ready to be president again as soon as we get to the bottom of this."

"Is that really necessary?" Mal asked, wiping his arm.

I sat down and leaned toward him. "Think about it, Mal. What if they never find the guy who sent the memo? It could be anyone who had a grudge against Jason. Or maybe Beebe really *did* send it, and the school is afraid that Jason's parents will sue. Who knows? But if they never do figure it out, Jason could pressure them to run the election again. And we might not win it next time. Sympathy for Jason is growing."

"I hear Dawn is his biggest fan these days," Mal said.

"She feels sorry for him," I said. "That's my point. He could get the sympathy vote. At Bloomfield, backlash is always right around the corner."

"You could be right," Mal said. "Okay, I'll do a macro and get the letter together."

"You've done enough, bud," I said. "I know I spaced out partway through the campaign. Let me handle it. Just show me the computer, and let my fingers fly."

"Okay," Mal said dubiously, as though he didn't trust me to write a decent letter.

"You can proof it," I said.

It didn't matter what the letter said. Mal would call up the macro that listed all the addresses, and I would find out exactly where Dawn lived.

Dawn lives on one of the big streets in Cicada Heights—Groveland. It's a wide avenue with big leafy oaks and huge houses. I knew she lived in a fancy condo, but I didn't think any developments were on that road. The condos must be hidden by trees. The Groveland Home Association probably won't allow condos to be seen from the road.

I started out near a rambling Tudor that could have parked an airplane in the garage. But the number was in the double digits. Dawn's number was 42. I was too high up on the street, so I kept cruising.

The numbers went down slowly, and soon, I was out of the familiar neighborhood and heading into a part of town I didn't know called Lower Cicada Heights. To tell you the truth, I wasn't even aware that people live in the Lower Heights. I thought you just got your car fixed there, or bought an air conditioner.

Groveland was no longer a leafy, wide street. It narrowed and was lined with shabby stores. The smooth asphalt turned into rutted pavement dotted with potholes from last winter.

I looked at the slip of paper again. The address must be wrong. My golden girl couldn't be from this neighborhood. It was one step over the line from a ghetto.

If I was on a wild-goose chase, I didn't

have much time. I knew Dawn was at cheerleading practice, but she'd probably be home by five. It was ten after four.

I bounced over some railroad tracks. Now a few houses lined one side of the street. They huddled together, as though for protection against the auto body shops.

Number 42 was painted sickly green. A pot of red geraniums sat on the concrete steps. I cruised ahead, then turned the corner. I parked and walked back.

The name on the mailbox was SEDARIS. This was getting weirder by the minute. I tried to remember what Dawn had told me about her parents. I realized she hadn't said much. But what kid talks about her parents? I just assumed her family was rolling in dough.

Then again, there was that rusty Ford Falcon. . . .

I headed down a concrete driveway that ran alongside the house. Tufts of grass stuck up through the cracks. I peered in the windows as I went, keeping an eye out for neighbors. I couldn't see anything. All of the shades were down.

Then, at the side window near the back, I hit the jackpot. I peeked through a pair of filmy flowered curtains with a gap between them. The room inside looked feminine, with a flowered bedspread and white furniture. And then I saw a Bloomfield High pennant.

I pushed against the window, and, to my surprise, it opened. It was easy to haul myself inside. Debbi was right—Dawn could definitely use better security.

It was Dawn's room, all right. A bulletin board held photos of all the Chosen Few. There were about five pictures of Dawn and Mark. If I took them down, then ripped them into tiny pieces and left them on the bed, would that clue her in to the fact that someone had been here?

A magazine was open on the small desk. Whole paragraphs of the article were highlighted with a yellow marker. The headline read, "'Luxe Is In—How to Achieve That Rich Girl Look Without Spending a Dime." There was a stack of fashion magazines on the desk. Yellow Post-it slips fluttered from the pages.

A sewing machine was the only other furniture. Clippings from magazines were stuck onto the wall with tape. I saw stacks of fabric, dyes, a box of buttons, needles and pins.

Dawn actually *sews*.

Dawn is *poor*.

I looked at my watch. Four-thirty. I was cutting it close. What if her parents came home from work early?

I looked around, searching for something to take. A book? The small stuffed chipmunk on her dresser? One of the birthday cards she had lined up on the top of the desk? I picked one up, a cheap one with one of those sappy sunsets on the front. *Thinking of you* was written in flowing script.

Inside, the card read: *Sunrise, sunset . . . through all the days of our lives, I hope to call you friend.*

Only "friend" was crossed out, and "daughter" was written above it. Down below was written, *Happy Birthday. Love, Dad*

P.S. hope to see you soon, honey!!!!

Talk about lame! He couldn't even manage

to pick out a real birthday card! And Dawn had never mentioned that her parents are divorced.

I heard a noise from the driveway, and I nearly jumped to the ceiling. I sprang to the window and peered out, keeping out of sight. A car was pulling into the driveway!

I glanced around frantically. I had to grab something—anything—*now*. I picked up a pink T-shirt that was lying across the bed. I stuffed it into the pocket of my jacket.

Now what? I couldn't leave by the window. Maybe there was a way out in the back. I could wait until the person entered the house, and . . .

The sound of the engine faded. I ran back to the window. To my relief, I saw that the car had only used the driveway to turn around.

But the call had been close enough for me. As soon as the car headed off, I lifted the window and climbed out again. I lowered it carefully. Then I ran down the driveway. I slowed my pace to a walk and headed to my car.

I lucked out. I found a Laundromat about

a half mile away. This time, I wouldn't give Hanigan any clues. I wouldn't use shoe polish.

I brought a shopping bag filled with what I needed inside. I dyed the shirt black with the dye I'd bought in a big supermarket at the other end of town. I used a rubber tub so that I wouldn't stain the sink. I didn't want anybody to have a reason to remember me. Nobody was in the Laundromat except the attendant, and he was engrossed in *Oprah*.

After I dyed the shirt, I slipped it into a pillowcase so that it wouldn't stain the inside of the dryer. I filled the dryer with coins and flipped the control to High. Fifteen minutes wouldn't be enough to dry the shirt completely, but I was running out of time.

While I watched the shirt tumble around in the dryer, I thought about what I'd found out about Dawn. Talk about hypocrites! She was lying to everyone. She had a secret life, too. We were more alike than I'd dreamed.

I took the shirt out of the dryer. I put it in

the envelope along with the note saying **SOMEDAY YOU WILL DIE.** I cleaned up any dye with paper towels from the shopping bag. Then I left.

I drove back to Dawn's and put the envelope in the mailbox. Then I drove away.

It was done. It had gone like clockwork. No one had seen me. No one would suspect.

This time, when Dawn came to me, scared and alone, I'd confess I was Lobo. I'd tell her how hard it is to have a secret you're afraid no one will understand. I'd tell her how that secret can grow so huge, you're afraid you'll never be able to get it out of you. I knew that she'd forgive me. She'd have to.

But thinking about that scene didn't make me feel triumphant or glad. I pulled over suddenly.

What was wrong? There was this strange feeling in my heart. An ache. I realized what it was. Sadness.

Dawn had so much to hide. I couldn't imagine the effort it must take to convince her friends every day that she lives in a deluxe condo and that her mother is a high-priced realtor. I couldn't imagine fashioning a wardrobe out of needles and pins and photos torn from magazines and telling everyone you bought your clothes in Chicago.

No wonder she'd felt sorry for Jason Polemus. No wonder she'd said, *They'll tear you apart if you don't fit in.*

Her room had been so sad. She wanted to fit in, and she'd do anything she could to make it happen.

Now I understood the strange things she'd said about being lonely, about being scared. Dawn wasn't a golden girl. She was more like me. And scaring her just didn't seem fair.

Sometimes in life, there is an "undo" key.

I circled back to Dawn's house. I parked a block away and hurried toward the mailbox. All I had to do was snatch it back, and run back to the car. Dawn would never know.

I had just reached her front walk when I heard my name called.

"Brian!"

I froze. Detective Hanigan was leaning

against a car across the street, reading a newspaper. She came toward me.

"She's not home yet," Detective Hanigan said, waving a stick of licorice at me. She held a pack in her hand. She held it out to me, but I shook my head.

"Oh," I said. "I guess she's still at practice. I'll take off, then."

"Actually, maybe you could help me," Hanigan said.

So even though Lobo screamed, *Bug off, Porky!* Brian Rittenhouse smiled and said, "Shoot."

"Thanks for getting me those transcripts, by the way," she said. She waved the licorice stick. "Trying to break my coffee jones. Anyway, I just need some help deciphering some more of these online names. Who's mallsurfrr?"

"Lauren Treadle," I said. "She's a cheerleader."

She took a bite of licorice. "Wildman is Chris Wilder," Hanigan said. "Newdawn is Dawn, and prez.bri is you. What about shyguy?"

"No idea," I said. I shifted nervously, then

forced my feet to stay still. I really didn't want to bump into Dawn.

"Have any more ideas about Lobo?" Hanigan asked. Her toffee-colored gaze was pleasant.

"Not a clue," I said.

"Word has it that you're trying to find out for Dawn Sedaris," Hanigan said.

"How did you know?" I blurted. I couldn't help it. "I mean, Dawn didn't want—"

"I read it in the *Scroll*, like everybody else," Hanigan said. "And Steffi Minor says she didn't write that article. As a matter of fact, she suggested that you did."

I chuckled in what I hoped was an offhand way. "Yeah, Steffi accused me. I don't know what she's thinking. I guess she just doesn't want to take responsibility for it."

"That's what Emily Talladega said."

I tried not to look surprised.

"Lots of stuff going on at Bloomfield," Hanigan remarked. "Things were sure different when I was there. Guess it was a simpler time."

"Listen, Detective Hanigan, I really have to go," I said. "My mom's expecting me."

Hanigan just kept chewing thoughtfully. "Sure. What do you think about the weird stuff going down at Bloomfield, Brian? I mean, you're a smart guy. Columns get written, memos get circulated, Dawn gets a black key chain in the mail. . . ." She tapped her nose with the licorice stick. "My nose tells me they're connected. What do you think?"

"I never thought about it," I said. "I mean, if it's a practical joker—"

"Pretty serious jokes," Hanigan said. She stuffed the licorice in her purse. "They hurt people. This prankster might not know it, but he or she is committing a crime."

"A crime?" I asked. "Which one?"

"I'll find something," Hanigan said. "'Cause I, for one, am not amused."

Her brown eyes suddenly looked shrewd. She gave me a hard glance. It felt like a two-ton slab of concrete had just whacked me on the head.

Then she patted my shoulder and grinned. "So keep me informed, will you? Now, I gotta run."

I said good-bye. I watched as she crossed

the road, got into her car, and drove away. I waited until she was out of sight. Then I dashed up to the mailbox, took out the envelope, and ran back to my car.

I sat in back of the wheel. I was breathing hard, and bathed in sweat.

I didn't care what Lobo thought. It was time to bail.

14//bad sneakers

"Brian, could I talk to you a minute?"

I kept my head down when I heard Emily Talladega's voice. I stared at her yellow socks. Today she wasn't wearing those signature boat-sized white sneakers, at least. She was wearing black loafers.

"I'm kind of busy," I said to her feet.

They shifted. "Just for a minute?"

She'd found me in the Media Resource Center. I was pretending to look up a video on Chinese culture for my social studies class. Actually, I was waiting for the bell so I could catch Dawn coming out of art history.

I looked up impatiently. Emily gave me a nervous smile. Her ginger hair was scraped back in a clip, and she was wearing a baggy peach sweater that did not exactly meld with her yellow socks. She was not what you'd call a vision.

"Can't we do this tomorrow?" I said. "Turkel is going to close the Media Center as soon as the bell rings, and I have to finish this. Or how about after school?"

Emily's cheeks were pink. "I have an appointment after school. I have to leave in, like, two minutes. And I just have a question."

With a show of impatience, I pushed aside my notes. "Okay. Shoot."

"Okay. Well. First of all, I know it could be awkward, my heading up the honor committee," she said. "I just wanted to make sure we were okay."

"Why wouldn't we be okay?" I said.

"Well, you know . . ." Emily's gaze was earnest. "I just wouldn't want you to . . . I mean, I'm going to be fair. That's all."

"Of course you'll be fair," I said. "I hope you'll be quick, too. Bloomfield needs leadership right now."

She nodded vigorously. "I agree. And I think you're the one to lead us, Brian. I mean, I voted for you. I don't think Jason has enough experience. He's a nice guy, but . . ."

"Thanks, Emily," I said. "You said you had a question?" The bell was about to ring, and I didn't want Emily to get in the way of my mad dash to Dawn.

"Right. I have to ask you something." Emily now looked truly uncomfortable. "In my capacity as chair, I have the original memo that was left in Principal Bigelow's box. There's a list at the bottom of all the student council officers that the memo should be sent to."

"I know," I said. "I got one in my mailbox. I was shocked when I read it. I knew it must have been a big mistake. I'm just sorry it got around the school."

Emily shifted from one foot to another. "Well, the thing is . . ."

"What is it, Emily?" I looked behind her at the clock.

"You're not on the carbon list," Emily blurted. "You see, I checked the names on the 'cc' list. 'cc' means 'carbon copy.'"

"I know what it means," I snapped.

"But you're not on it," she said. "And

you got a copy. So I just noticed it and wondered . . . why."

How could I have been so stupid? I'd left myself off the list! I had been focusing on everyone who'd needed to get it. No wonder the printer hadn't printed out enough copies!

I wanted to kick myself all around the Resource Center, but Emily was gazing at me.

"I don't know why I'm not on the list," I said. "I have no idea. Why should I? I got a copy. That's all I know." Then a thought occurred to me. Maybe Emily was bluffing, trying to get me to confess. "Are you sure I'm not on the list?"

"Well, I looked at the memo," Emily said.

"Did you check the computer?" I asked.

"Well, no," Emily said. "But—"

"Maybe something happened, some glitch," I said. "My name could have dropped to the next page, and Beebe didn't print it. Maybe you should check the original file on the hard drive."

And maybe I can get to it before you do.

She'd already told me she had an appointment outside school. I could do it after school today.

"I'll do that, I guess," Emily said. "That's a good idea. Maybe after my appointment."

The bell rang. I heard doors opening, and students rushing out into the hallway. I would miss Dawn. But I had worse problems.

"Well, if that's it—" Maybe there was still time to catch Dawn at her locker, if Emily would just shut up.

"It's not. I've seen you talking to that Detective Hanigan," Emily said. "Do the police think that whoever sent that key chain to Dawn Sedaris was a practical joker?"

"They're not sure," I said. "Why?"

Emily reached into her canvas tote bag. She plucked out a black sneaker. "Because I got this in the mail," she said in a low tone.

I stared at it.

"It used to be white," she said.

I'll say it did. What was going on? I didn't do this!

So who did?

"I know, I was shocked, too," Emily said. "I mean, who would want to scare me? Not

exactly a challenge. I'm such an easy target."
She smiled ruefully. "Everything scares me.
Thunderstorms, traffic, hamburgers that
look too rare. Dentists. I'm scared right now
because I'm heading to Dr. Weinstock's."
She looked at the sneaker. "It came with that
same note. 'Someday you will die. Signed,
the 24 Point Club.' Freaked me out."

I stared at her. My mind was blank.
Can't help you, Em. I'm freaked, too.

I left school as usual and drove around to
kill time. Then I went to a mini mall near
school that had a pizzeria, a coffee shop,
and a used CD store, all Bloomfield High
hangouts. If things went wrong, and Emily
suspected that I'd tampered with Mrs.
Beebe's hard drive, I would have a sort-of
alibi. I could say I'd been at the mini mall,
and chances were that she'd find at least a
few kids who could confirm that they had
seen my car. They would remember seeing
me, but they wouldn't be able to exactly
pinpoint the time.

I bought a few CDs and got a slice of
pizza. I talked to a few kids so they'd

remember me. Then I went out the back door of the pizzeria and walked back to school. My head was still buzzing with the sight of that black sneaker. Had I kicked off something that was now out of control? Had I resurrected some psycho mentality?

It all had to end. After today, I promised myself, I would banish Lobo forever.

I slipped into the side door of the old wing. I used the east stairs, the ones kids didn't use much. I didn't see anyone. Good. It would be much better for me if nobody knew I was there.

I killed some extra time in the student council office. But I couldn't wait very long. Emily could head back at any time. What if her dentist appointment was only a cleaning? She had pretty nice teeth. It might not take very long. And she was probably anxious to get to Mrs. Beebe's computer.

I had to sneak down there before the school was empty. It was the only way.

The halls were empty now. I heard the clang of the custodian's bucket as he headed into the fourth-floor bathrooms. I started down the east stairs.

But I heard footsteps heading toward me, and voices, so I had to duck out on the third floor and head down the hall. As I was passing the offices of the *Scroll,* I looked in the window. I didn't think Emily was around, but if she was at school, that was one place she'd be.

The office was dark, though. But after a second, I made out the shape of a person sitting, staring into space. It was Mark Skeeter.

Why was he sitting in the dark, all alone?

Just then, he looked up. It was too late to duck out. With a sigh, he got up and came to the door. He opened it. So much for all my subterfuge.

He kept his face down. "What is it, Brian?"

"I was looking for Emily," I said. Sometimes, the truth works as well as a lie.

"She's not here," he said. He sniffed. Suddenly, I wondered if I'd caught him crying. Mark Skeeter? "I'm about to close up. I'll tell her you came by. It's time for me to head home, anyway." Mark slipped out and shut the door behind him.

"Mark, why are you sitting in the dark all alone?" I asked. I couldn't help it.

"I'm moody," he said, and walked away.

I backed away and hurried toward the west staircase. It was just bad luck that Mark had seen me. But I still had to break into Beebe's computer today.

I headed across the catwalk into the new wing and took the stairs down to the first floor. Even though my alibi was pretty much blown, I still didn't want to be seen heading for the administration offices. If I went across the first floor and crossed the covered walkway back to the old wing, I might make it without being seen again.

I hit the ground floor and started toward the east door. As I was walking by the gym, I heard the sound of chanting. *"Wolf Wolf Wolv-erine."* The cheerleaders were practicing, and the gym door was wide open. I had to pass it, or double back and go up the stairs again to the second floor to take the catwalk. This was getting way complicated. Not to mention aerobically challenging.

I decided to take a chance. But naturally, as I passed, I had to sneak a peek into the gym. What guy wouldn't sneak a peek at cheerleaders bouncing around in little red skirts?

It was just bad luck that Dawn caught my eye as I walked past. Maybe I should have just taken out an ad in the *Scroll: Brian Rittenhouse is going to tamper with Beebe computer files right after school!*

Dawn motioned at me to wait. With a quick glance at Coach Clampett, she dashed through the cartwheeling team to the bleachers. She picked up her backpack and hurried out into the hall, closing the gym door behind her.

"What's the matter?" I asked.

Dawn reached into the backpack. She withdrew a tiny stuffed animal. With a jolt, I realized it was the chipmunk I'd seen on her dresser. Only now it was black.

Not another one! Who *was* this guy? I felt chilled. There really was a psycho at Bloomfield. And it wasn't me!

I took it from her. "A chipmunk? Where did you get it?"

"It's mine," Dawn said grimly. "It's not a chipmunk, it's a mouse. It used to be cute.

Somebody sent this . . . thing to me."

I gazed at her curiously. This time, she didn't seem scared. She looked angry.

"With a note?"

She nodded. "And I know who it is."

"You do?"

Dawn snatched it back and stuffed it into her backpack. "That rat."

"I thought it was a mouse."

She looked at me furiously. "Mark Skeeter! That's who did it. He's behind all of it."

I thought of Mark sitting in the dark upstairs. "Why do you think it's Mark?"

"He's the only one who knows where I live, first of all," Dawn said. She flushed. "He's been there. And he has a key! I had to give him one once, when he helped my mother out. He moved her couch in his pickup. I gave him a key. Don't you see? He probably duplicated it! Or when he stole my key ring, he could have made a copy—"

Now why didn't I think of that?

"—he has my locker combination. It's the same as last year's. He betrayed me, Brian! And he was the one person—" Her voice choked, and she stopped.

"I don't know about this," I said.

"Plus, the *mouse*," Dawn said, swiping angrily at a stray strand of golden hair. "Mark gave me that mouse. He won it at a carnival last summer. He's trying to tell me that his love for me is dead, too."

"Dawn, it sounds like it could be true," I said cautiously. "But you still could be leaping to conclu—"

"I think he could be the ringleader of the 24 Point Club, too," Dawn said rapidly. She grabbed my arm. "Think about it, Brian. Mark won a statewide journalism award last year. Why? Because of his reporting on the club. But what if he *created* the news so that he'd have something to write about? He's very ambitious. And that whole thing that happened with us last year? He loved me, I know he did. So why did he reject me? I mean, that just doesn't happen, does it? It was because he was *guilty*."

Gee, I thought it was because he couldn't forgive you for the way you dumped him as soon as Jamie Fletcher asked you out.

"Look, Dawn," I said. "I'm not saying you're wrong. You could be right. But if I were you, I wouldn't tell anyone else. Let's keep it between us, because—"

"Oh, I already told him," Dawn said, flipping her hair behind her shoulder. "Do you think I'd let him get away with this?"

"What did he say?"

She snorted. "He told me he didn't do it, of course. And he acted all hurt that I'd even suggest it, okay? Like I'd believe him! He said he loved me, but he didn't want to love me. I mean, that's pretty weird, don't you think?"

"Maybe he was telling the truth," I said. "I mean about not sending the chip—the mouse."

"Brian, I'm telling you, I'm right!" Dawn cried. "It has to be him, because of the name. It totally makes sense—"

"Miss Sedaris!"

Coach Clampett stood, petite and muscular, in the doorway. She rolled her whistle around in her fingers. "Inside."

"But I was just telling—"

"Inside. Or you're benched. Choose." Perhaps I should mention at this juncture that Coach Clampett is also occasionally known as the Terminator?

"I'll call you," Dawn whispered, and slipped back into the gym.

Mark Skeeter?

I remembered his face when he'd come to the door. How he'd sat in the dark, not moving. I wasn't his biggest fan, but I still couldn't connect Mark with the kind of goons who'd let a girl drown, or scare her half to death.

And I still had a job to do. I hurried toward the back stairs, with the chant *Wolf Wolf Wolv-er-ine* sounding in my brain.

15//dark hallways

When I hit the administration offices, I did a careful area recon. The custodian was cleaning the bathroom. I hung out in an empty classroom until he finished. But when I peeked out, he was rolling the cart toward the administration offices.

I hit my fist against the wall. Now I'd have to wait until he'd finished. And judging by the time he'd taken to clean the bathroom, I could be here forever.

But the guy unlocked the office—I couldn't have gotten in, anyway—and left the cart standing outside. He patted his front pocket, then headed toward the stairs.

It didn't take Sherlock Holmes to figure out that he was ducking out for a smoke.

I sped out of the classroom and headed down the dim hallway. I'd have to work fast.

I hurried into Mrs. Beebe's dark office. I booted up her computer. This time, I knew where to look for the right file, so it only took a few seconds.

I checked the memo. My name wasn't on the carbon list. Emily hadn't been bluffing.

But I couldn't add my name, I decided. That would look suspicious, especially since Emily had just talked to me. Instead, I deleted the entire memo. That might look suspicious, too, but Mrs. Beebe isn't the most computer literate person. It might make sense that she wouldn't back up her files.

I heard the rattle of the custodian's cart. He was in the outer office. I tried Mrs. Beebe's other door. Locked.

I peered out through a crack in the door. The custodian was leaning over, emptying the trash into a giant garbage bag. There was an overflowing can in the far corner. He headed there next.

As soon as he bent over, his back to the door, I quietly crossed the space, opened the door, and eased out of the room.

Perspiration sprinkled my forehead. I wiped my hands on my jeans. Close call.

I crossed back into the new wing so that I could swing by the gym and talk to Dawn. But when I got there, it was dark. The cheerleaders had all gone.

I felt really let down, and I wasn't sure why. I stood for a minute, staring into the empty gym.

The truth was, I was tired. Tired of juggling Lobo and Brian. Tired of worrying about Hanigan and Emily and the mysterious ringleader of the 24 Point Club. I was holding on to my position at Bloomfield by my fingernails. They were about to rip off from the strain.

I was ready to tell Dawn I was Lobo.

I was tired of lying, and sneaking around. I had taken care of the steroid memo. No one would be able to trace it to me. So I'd get away with it, and maybe I wouldn't deserve to. But at least I could do one thing right. I could come clean with Dawn. I could be . . . well, honest.

Maybe she hadn't left school yet. It was chilly today, so she definitely had a coat. Maybe she'd left it in her locker during practice.

I reversed direction and took the steps two at a time. Already, I was feeling better. Just making the decision made me feel that everything would be okay.

When I hit the fourth floor, the hallway was empty. No Dawn. No spill of golden hair, no dark blue eyes turning me into a Gummi Bear left on the dashboard until it melts.

How would I be able to tell her, face-to-face? I could barely form sentences around her. And this thing had to be finessed. Maybe I could send Mal as my representative. Didn't they do that kind of stuff in the Middle Ages?

E-mail. I had to do it by e-mail. I would send her a message that I could word carefully. I could say exactly the right thing. Then I could hand her my computer, tell her she had a message from Lobo, and scoot.

I headed toward my locker. I'd get my notebook and compose the letter at home. I'd send it before I lost my nerve.

I was halfway down the hall when the lights went out.

Don't panic. The lights just went out. Big

deal. Maybe they're on a timer. Or maybe the custodian was at the other end of the hallway, and he'd finished mopping.

I waited until my eyes adjusted to the darkness. When I could make out the shadowy doorways, I started toward my locker. It was farther down the hall than Dawn's. I could work the lock blindfolded. I had the same one since sophomore year.

The stillness rushed against my ears. I'd stayed late at school plenty of times, but somehow, I felt creeped out. It was the lights shutting off so quickly. I tried not to think about a demented psycho on the loose. I tried not to picture Mark Skeeter coming up from behind me with a baseball bat.

Relax. He's not athletic. He'd probably miss.

But the sooner I was out of here, the better.

I was just starting to spin the lock when I thought I heard a soft yell. It was so faint, I wasn't sure what I'd heard. It sounded as though it had come from farther down the hall, or maybe outside on the catwalk. I listened and thought I heard scuffling noises. And a thump.

"Hello?" I called. Nothing.

Okay. Here's the part where I should have turned and run, not walked, to the nearest exit. But I didn't. Somewhere I was able to access this tiny brave part of myself, and I walked *toward* the noise. It was my curiosity. If something was going on, and Mark Skeeter was around, I would have proof that Dawn was right.

I headed cautiously down the hall. Every hair on my body was standing at attention. I had this totally eerie feeling of dread. All I wanted to do was turn around and go home. But I kept on moving.

I pressed my face against the window of each classroom door. My eyes had adjusted to the darkness. I could make out shadowy desks, an abandoned umbrella, a sweater left on a chair.

I turned the corner and came to the door that led to the catwalk. To my right, on the wall, was a wall switch. All of the lights had been switched off.

I eased open the door. The darkness pressed against the windows. The catwalk was empty, as far as I could see.

I walked out and peered toward the old wing. Not even a shadow flickered. Whoever had made the noise was gone.

I looked out the window, toward the exterior stairs. I didn't see anyone running down, or across the quad. But I caught a flash of yellow on the ground way below.

I pushed open the door to the staircase. The crisp air smelled like autumn—dead leaves and damp earth. I stood on the landing. I peered over the railing.

Yellow socks. Emily Talladega's yellow socks. She lay on the concrete walkway four stories below. One leg was twisted at a funny angle. Something dark was pooling around her head.

Something dark . . . blood.

"Emily?" I whispered. Which was stupid, because even if she were alive, she couldn't possibly hear me. And Emily looked very dead.

A phone. I need a phone.

My legs didn't feel like they could move, but I turned from the railing. I heard a window opening to the right of me. Good—the custodian. He could call—

A head popped out of the window in the classroom two doors down. It was Hanigan. She looked down at Emily. Then she looked up at me, standing by the railing.

We stared at each other for a split second. Nobody moved.

She put a hand out, meaning, *stay there.* Her head jerked inside.

I didn't hesitate. I ran.

16//for real

I pounded down the catwalk stairs and jumped the last three to solid ground. I heard Hanigan yelling above me, but I hit the walk and kept on going. I headed away from Emily's body. I didn't even look at it.

The cool air hit the sweat that soaked my shirt. I was shaking as I ran. I expected Hanigan to shoot me in the back, or chase after me.

But when I took a minute to look back, there was no one behind me.

I was no Jason Polemus, so I ran out of breath in an embarrassingly short period of time. I finally stopped in the shadow of the stadium. I bent over, trying to catch my breath. My brain was working at hyper-speed.

Of course Hanigan didn't have to chase

me. She'd seen me. She'd been to my house. All she had to do was call in my name and address. Where could I run to?

But why did I run in the first place?

There were a couple of answers to that question. The first one was that I was an idiot. But I don't think I even have to bring that one up.

I panicked, sure. The situation didn't look good, as far as innocence goes. But incredibly enough, my brain had functioned quickly and efficiently.

I was guilty. Not of pushing Emily over a railing. But maybe all the stupid stuff I'd done—sending Dawn that key chain, for starters—had brought the psycho out of hiding. I was responsible.

And all the evidence pointed to me.

If I was caught, Hanigan would think she'd solved the case. And that meant that the psycho was still out there. Because someone had pushed Emily Talladega off that catwalk.

Which meant that Dawn was in danger. Serious danger.

I heard the wail of a siren. A few

moments later, I caught the white blur of the rescue vehicle.

I pressed back against the shadows as a cop car flew by. I knew another car had probably been dispatched to my house. And the streets were probably already being searched, plus all the usual teenage hang-outs. It wouldn't take them long to find my car. I couldn't go there.

I had nowhere to go and no way to get there. So I went to the only place I could think of, and probably the only place they wouldn't think of searching.

The side door to the old wing was open. I figured that the custodian left it open for his cigarette breaks. I took the east stairs two at a time. I wanted to get as far away from the activity as possible.

The third floor was dark and quiet. I tip-toed to the door of the *Scroll* office. I knew they had a phone. And I remembered that Mark hadn't locked the door behind him when I'd surprised him sitting in the dark.

Before he'd pushed Emily over?

I closed the door softly behind me.

Someone's sweatshirt had been left on a chair, and I slipped it on. I was still shaking.

I sat down at Mark's desk. I ran my hands along the arms of the chair. I tried to picture Mark Skeeter pushing Emily over a railing. I couldn't. Mark isn't my favorite person, but if I push aside my jealousy, I have to admit that I've always thought of him as a good guy. But even good guys can freak out. Wasn't I proof of that? You can want something so much that you'll do anything to get it. Because if you don't have it, you feel like you'll just disappear.

Somebody was still out there. Somebody who headed up the 24 Point Club. I had to figure out who it was before I was thrown in jail.

What had Dawn said? *If it's Mark, the name totally makes sense.*

I looked around the office. Everyone always figured that 24 points had something to do with football. Or maybe the members were assigned points for every time they hassled someone.

But Dawn must have figured something else out. What else has 24 points? And what would it have to do with Mark?

I sat there for a minute, trying to think, but I was wasting time. I needed help. I needed the smartest person I knew. I dialed Mal's number.

I got his dad. He already sounded as though he'd downed his first cocktail.

"Brian? Is that you? What the—what's going on? The police were just here, looking for you. Where's Mal? He's not home. What's he done now?" Mr. Bouchard bellowed into the phone.

It was worse than I'd thought. They'd already come looking for me at Mal's!

"He hasn't done anything, Mr. Bouchard," I said. "There . . . was a vandal at school, and they're checking anyone who was there at the time. I have to go now."

I hung up and dialed Mal's cell phone number. He picked it up on the first ring.

"It's me, bud," I said.

"Brian! Where are you, bud? Something freaky is going on. The police were at my house, man! I split. My dad didn't know I was there. I'm in my car."

"Something freaky is right," I said. "Mal, Emily Talladega just got pushed over a railing. The police think I did it!"

"That's crazy," Mal said. "Are you sure?"

I rolled my eyes. Was I *sure?* I would make this stuff up? "Of course I'm sure!" I hissed.

"Okay, okay, calm down," Mal said.

I pushed aside Mark's papers and rested my forehead on the desk. "Oh, I'm totally calm," I said, my mouth against the phone. "The police think I'm a murderer. Not to mention the ringleader of the 24 Point Club."

"The 24 Point Club?" Mal's voice boomed through the receiver. "What do they have to do with it?"

But I didn't answer. I slowly raised my head. I had pushed aside page proofs for the *Scroll*, and they were literally under my nose. I stared at them.

And, suddenly, things clicked into place.

I knew what Dawn meant now about the name of the club. And maybe the name gave me a clue to finding out who the psycho was for sure.

"Brian? Come in, buddy. I'm losing you. This cell—"

"It's not the cell," I said. "I think I just got it, Mal. I think I just figured out what the 24 Point Club is all about. And I think I know who the ringleader is."

"You do?"

"You have to get Dawn," I said.

"*Dawn?* I have to get Dawn? What does she have to do with it?" Mal shouted. "Keep this between us, bud. Tell me where you are. I can take care of this. I'll pick you up. We'll talk about all this. All night, if we have to. You're my bud, man!"

Mal sounded frantic, as if he thought I was crazy. Maybe I was.

Mal had prodded and pushed me into campaigns. He'd stayed up until three A.M. writing campaign literature. He had sacrificed and used his brilliant brain to make sure that we weren't outcasts in a school that eats nerds for breakfast.

But I'd never felt more grateful to him than at this moment. He was willing to go to the mat for me, no matter what.

"Mal, you're the best," I said. "That's why I'm asking you to do this for me. It is seriously and totally important. Dawn could be in real danger. You've got to go to her house and pick her up. Take her somewhere safe, or just drive around and keep out of sight." I picked up the page proofs and stared at them. I might have figured out the name, but I still had more brain work to do.

"Brian, where are—"

"I've got to go," I said. "I'll be in touch."

I hung up the phone while Mal was still talking. I stared at the page proofs. I didn't understand some of the proofreading symbols. But next to a headline, someone had written in red pencil *24 point type.*

Headlines! It had to do with headlines!

I turned on Mark's computer and got to work.

First, I looked up one of the articles that Mark wrote about the 24 Point Club, when it was still breaking news. I didn't remember the code numbers for each of the guys who were caught.

I wrote them down:

Jamie Fletcher = 8
Greg Littlejohn = 9
Kyle Woodham = 5
David Rollins = 3

Then I wrote down a 2 and circled it. That was the possible code number of the ringleader. Now it was time to test my theory.

I knew that the *Scroll* is linked to the archive files of the town paper. I typed in "Jamie Fletcher," then limited the search to the football season, before he was arrested.

The search engine listed fifteen articles in which he was mentioned. In eight of them, Jamie's name was in the headline, such as "Fletcher Pass Nails Winning TD" and "Fletcher Makes Fourth Down, Miracles Happen."

All in twenty-four-point type.

I did a search on Greg Littlejohn. Eleven articles popped up. His name was in the headline nine times.

Greg and Jamie had been the stars of the team. Kyle was next in line. He was in five headlines. David had only three mentions. He'd been a defensive end.

I sat at the desk, thinking. What a bunch of idiots. They actually counted how many times they were in a headline in the town paper. That meant the code names had to change from week to week. No wonder nobody had been able to figure it out.

Maybe that's how the whole thing had started—maybe they had gotten used to the glory. Maybe they wanted to see themselves in the paper again, even if nobody knew it was them. So they had threatened people and harassed them. It was a stupid game.

I did a search on Mark Skeeter. His name came up once, for the time he won that journalism award. But his name wasn't even in the headline. In Cicada Heights, being a good journalist is nothing compared to passing a ball.

Which meant that Mark wasn't 2.

But Dawn was still in danger. I had to figure out who 2 was! I felt as though I were trapped in some weird James Bond flick.

Then I remembered something stupid. I hadn't given Dawn's address to Mal! And I hadn't told him I was here. He was probably afraid to go back to his house. That's the only place he could access that macro program and find out where she lives.

I picked up the phone and dialed Mal's cell phone. It rang and rang. He hadn't turned on his voice mail. Annoyed, I hung up. Mal knew I would be calling back!

I tried Dawn's number. Her mother answered.

"Mrs. Sedaris? This is a classmate of Dawn's, Brian Rittenhouse. Is she there?"

"I'm sorry, Brian. Dawn went out," her mom said. "Can I leave a message?"

"Do you know who she left with?" I asked. "It's really important. I was supposed to hook up with her later. . . ."

"She left with someone named Malcolm," Mrs. Sedaris said. "I didn't catch his last name, sweetie. Should I—"

"That's okay," I said. "I'll find them."

I hung up. I stared at the phone. How had Mal found Dawn? How had he known her address? I'd had to break into school files to get it.

I checked my watch. He'd gotten there awfully fast. I'd hung up barely ten minutes ago.

Keep this between us, bud. Tell me where you are. I can take care of this. I'll pick you up. We'll talk about all this. All night, if we have to.

Had I misinterpreted Mal's tone? Maybe it wasn't loyalty. Maybe it was panic.

Was Mal afraid that I knew *he* was the ringleader?

Crazy thoughts. I was alone, and in trouble, and my brain was fried. Mal as the head of a club full of jocks? Mal is probably the only student, aside from a couple of freaks in the Art Club, who never goes to games.

And what does Mal know about proof-reader's marks?

Plenty. He'd made the mock-up of the *Scroll* last year to win me the presidency.

I swung the chair around to face the computer screen. I couldn't believe I was doing this. Maybe I was doing it just to get rid of that little shadow of a doubt. Just so I could move on.

I slowly typed out Mal's name in the search engine. The computer told me it was searching. I stared at the screen. Every muscle was tense.

Two articles popped up.

BLOOMFIELD HIGH STUDENT MALCOLM BOUCHARD WINS CHICAGO SCIENCE FAIR

BOUCHARD DONATES PRIZE MONEY TO SUICIDE PREVENTION HOT LINE

Two headlines. My hands curled into fists. I beat them against my legs.

It couldn't be Mal. Not Mal, with his hound dog face, his stone-cold brilliant brain, his tragic dark eyes, his resentment of the popularity ranking at Bloomfield High, his contempt for jocks and Almosts and Nevers and even Voids . . . .

Mal, it can't be you. It can't.

It could be plenty of other people. But where was Mal? Now I had to talk to him. I dialed the cell again. It rang and rang. Each ring was like a stab in the heart.

"Pick up, Mal," I muttered. "Pick up!"

But the phone kept on ringing.

18//hide in plain sight

I needed to see him, face-to-face. I needed
him to tell me that it wasn't him. Then we'd
run some kind of super computer program
to see who else at Bloomfield had gotten
mentioned in a headline twice last year during a three-and-a-half-month period.

And then we'd find the *real* psycho.

I went to the dark window and peered
out. I couldn't see the front of the school
from these windows, but I could see the
bounce of reflected red light off the building. That meant there were still police cars
parked in front.

The cops were probably using the catwalk stairs to get back and forth to their
cars. I had a pretty good chance of sneaking out the way I'd come. The only problem was that there were probably way

more cops now. It would be safer to wait.

But I couldn't wait.

I took the dark east stairs to the ground floor. I pushed open the door cautiously. I was around the corner, on the side of the building. I could hear the police radios, but the cars were pulled up in front. No one was around.

Hugging the wall, I made my way along the side toward the back. Here is where it got tricky. The police would be on the cat-walk, and I would have to dash across the gap between the buildings to get to the street.

It was dark. They'd be busy working up there, gathering evidence to convict me. They might not see me.

I risked a peek above. Two cops were up on the fourth-floor landing. They were bent over, doing something at the railing. Their backs were to me. Three police cars were parked near the area where Emily had land-ed. I could see the outline of her body. One cop leaning against the car, speaking into the radio. His back was also to me.

I sprang forward, ready to close the distance.

But I heard the crackle of another radio. Coming toward me. My heart slammed against my chest, and I jumped back into the shadow of the building just in time.

It was Hanigan. She walked under the catwalks with another cop in plain clothes.

She touched his arm, and they stopped. They were only inches from me, and I could hear every word she said.

"Listen, Follette, I just got a call from Berlinger at the hospital. The kid's not going to make it. She's in a coma, but the doctors say she's not going to wake up. So as far as I'm concerned, this is a possible murder investigation. I want you to lean on the uniforms, forensics, everybody—no mistakes."

"Poor kid," Follette said. "What is she, seventeen?"

"Yeah," Hanigan said. "I could really use some coffee right now."

"I'll send Kass for some. He only gets in the way, anyway."

Hanigan snorted a laugh, and they moved on. I let out the breath I was holding.

Emily was still alive. But she wasn't going to make it.

Sorry, Emily. I'll think about you later. Right now I've got to get out of here.

As soon as Hanigan and Follette disappeared into the building, I took off.

I had to be careful. I couldn't run. I had to keep my steps slow and easy, trying to look like I was just out for a stroll. I stayed in the shadows as much as I could. I found the evening paper lying on a lawn and I took it, adding theft to my list of crimes. If I saw a cop car, I would head up the nearest driveway, pretending I'd just come out for the paper.

Without a car, I couldn't cruise, looking for Mal. I had to figure out where he would go. Where would he feel safe? Where would he think no one would look?

The answer came to me, not in a flash, but quietly, like a truth I knew in my heart.

If what I suspected was true, there was only one place. The place where his world had blown apart one crisp fall afternoon. The place where everything had spun out of control, and nothing had made sense anymore. Where life had tapped Mal on the shoulder and said, *Take that!*—and beaten him into the ground.

"Hi Mom, I'm home!" And you walk in on Mom, her eyes wide open, and her head at this funny angle . . . all because she was hanging a curtain, and she lost her balance for a split second, and the brick floor came rushing up at her before she'd even had time to think *oops!*

I jogged up Mal's long, curving drive-way. Mal's Explorer wasn't parked in front of the garage. But if he wanted me to think he wasn't home, he wouldn't park there. He'd park on the street behind the house and make his way through the backyard.

I ran across the dark, wet grass, past the covered swimming pool and down the long, sloping lawn. Down past what used to be Mrs. Bouchard's rose garden. Now it was just weeds.

The bunker looked dark and abandoned. I couldn't see any lights. But as I came closer, I saw that the same heavy, dark curtains were still at the windows. A pencil-thin ray of light shone through a crack.

Moving slowly and quietly, I eased next

to the front door. I pressed my ear against the wood. I thought I heard someone talking.

What now?

I had to know if Mal and Dawn were in there. But I couldn't tell if it was Mal's voice. And I couldn't hear Dawn.

I put my hand on the knob. I turned it, millimeter by millimeter, as slowly and quietly as I could.

But suddenly, the knob was yanked out of my hand, and the door swung open. I blinked at the sudden light.

Mal stood in front of me, smiling broadly.

"Brian! Hey, bud! We've been waiting for you!"

I took a step forward, relieved by his grin. I'd been an idiot. Everything was okay. Mal was still Mal. My bud.

Then I saw Dawn. She sat in a chair. Her face looked different, taut and distorted, and I realized it was because she was terrified.

I looked back at Mal. And that's when I saw the gun.

Mal's jaw dropped, and he bulged out his eyes in a comical imitation of me.

"Well, d-uh!" he said.

He grabbed me by the shirt collar, yanked me inside, then slammed the door closed with his foot.

He was wearing those latex gloves that dentists wear. He tapped the barrel of the gun gently against his lips. "Let me see . . . ," he said. "Mal has a gun! He's keeping Dawn captive! What I could hardly dare to believe must be right! He *is* the 24 Point Club ringleader!"

"Are you all right?" I said to Dawn.

She nodded. "He's crazy," she whispered to me.

Mal cupped his hand behind his ear. "Excuse me? I'm, like, standing right here,

Dawnie, okay? It's like, I can, like, *hear you!*" he suddenly roared.

Dawn shrank back against the chair. "I'm scared," she whispered.

Mal bent down, eye level with her. He ran the gun down her temple and down her cheek. "Lions and tigers and bears, oh my!" he crooned.

Dawn whimpered. A tear rolled down her cheek.

Mal had always been smarter than me. His brain was quick and agile.

But now, I knew I had to get up to speed, fast. I had to be as smart as he was. Smarter. Quicker.

"Hey, Mal," I said softly. "I walked into the middle of this movie, bud. I mean, the last time I saw you, you were a seminormal teen. Since when did you become a homicidal maniac?"

Mal wheeled around, chuckling. Dawn slumped back against the chair. At least I'd gotten him to move the gun away from her face.

"Good one, bud. Take it light, right?" There was a sheen of perspiration on his face.

"Just clue me in," I said. "The 24 Point Club. I'm in a state of shock, bud. Were you really hanging out with jocks?"

Mal laughed. "Not hanging. Leading. They were following me."

I wondered how to play this. Maybe if I was skeptical, Mal would spill. He hates it when I doubt him.

"Let me grasp this scenario," I said. "The coolest guys at school let you lead them? Why am I having trouble with this concept?"

Mal's face grew red. "Because no matter how much I've done for you, you've always underestimated me, bud!"

"So enlighten me," I said. "How did you become the Pied Piper of Jockdom?"

"It started one day after school last year," Mal said. "It was dark when I finally left." He whipped around and glared at me. "Working on *your* campaign for prez, I might add. They surrounded me in the parking lot. Started hassling me. Calling me a loser and dork—you know, the usual jock wit. So instead of cowering, I turned it around." Mal smiled. "I made them turn on each other."

"That probably wasn't too hard," I said.

"You're right, bud. It wasn't hard. Hormones were pumping. We got into a discussion of who the Wolverines could do without and still win the championship. Jamie and Greg were rivals, you know. They started out kidding each other, but then it got nasty. So I suggested a game."

"Which was—"

"A point for every time their names were in a headline. They always put the most valuable player in the headline when they talk about a game." Mal waved the gun. "And *voilà*, as Madame Zwerling would say. The 24 Point Club was born. Perfectly harmless."

"Except someone got killed!" Dawn spat out.

"Whoa, a remark from the peanut gallery," Mal said, without turning. "Football is a blood sport. You may remember how Greg and Jamie suddenly started playing more aggressively. One might even say . . . illegally. And Coach Cappistrano never said a word. He knew his job depended on the Wolverines staying champions."

I remembered that season. It was high in

injuries. Especially for the other teams. But nobody cared. We were winning.

"Those guys have been involved in competitive sports since they could walk," Mal said. "T-ball, Little League, soccer, you name it. They're used to the pack mentality. A good loser is still a loser, right? It's the American Way."

"So why did they go outside the football field?" I asked. "Why did they turn into a gang?"

Mal sighed. "Greg and Jamie got crazed about who was first. There was a dispute about headlines. Greg was in one before the season, which would have tied them. Jamie said it didn't count. So they decided to keep themselves in the headlines. I mean, that's how it started. I think the dispute was an excuse. I think they missed the glory. So Greg came up with this scheme to scare Jenny Rigorski just for fun. They made the front page, remember?"

"For torturing some girl?" Dawn asked. "They thought that was *cool?*"

"Major cool," Mal said. "Did I say they had brains?"

"So what happened with the coach?" I asked. "Were you there?"

"I was at the meeting in the parking lot," Mal said. "Cappy was a dork. He started talking about giving ourselves up. He mentioned the word 'therapy,' bud. To those apes! Their idea of self-awareness is checking their blow-dry job in a mirror. Cappy gave us twenty-four hours to turn ourselves in. So after he left, we discussed what to do. It was Greg who said we should waste him. I told the guys to chill. I figured maybe I could get something on the coach—maybe in his credit records, or something. Something to blackmail him on. Then we'd just swear that we'd disband, and we'd be even."

"So what happened?"

"I left first, to get to the computer. But I guess Greg and Jamie freaked. Kyle is a moron, so he went along. And David can be talked into anything, because he's a secret wimp." Mal rubbed his arms, as though he were cold. "We were supposed to meet later that night, but nobody showed up. I knew something was up. I went looking for them.

I got to Cappy's house just as he opened the door."

"Did you see them do it?"

He nodded. "Greg had the gun. But they were all in on it. Cappy looked mighty surprised, and then . . . boom!" Mal made the noise of a gunshot. Dawn jumped.

Mal's arm dropped, the one with the gun. If I rushed him, could I get it? Mal and I are about equal in the brute strength department. We both don't have much. He is large and lumpy, and I am thin and flabby.

"I could have killed them myself," Mal said. "Just being implicated could completely ruin my future career in politics. So we got out of there and went back to the parking lot. We talked about what to do. I said I'd get rid of the gun. Nobody had seen us drive up. Lucky for those morons that Coach lived on that dead end. We thought we'd be okay. I guess the police are smarter than we think."

"You're a monster," Dawn said to him. "You're talking about *killing* someone, okay? And you're only thinking about how it's going to look?"

Mal crossed the room in two lar?
strides. I moved a step forward, but h?
snapped, "Remember who has the gun,
Brian," and I stopped. I kept my eyes on
Dawn, reassuring her. I didn't think Mal
would do something stupid.

At least not yet. Not until he finished
telling the story.

He knelt in front of her chair. He didn't
point the gun at her this time, but he kept it
loosely hanging from his hand, in her sight
line.

"Listen to Little Miss Popularity," he
said. "You think you're better than me, little girl? You'd lick the halls of Bloomfield
clean with your *tongue* if it meant you could
be prom queen. You lie just by breathing."
Mal mimicked Dawn, putting on a Valley
Girl accent. "I, like, wrecked my dad's
Jaguar last year, and he freaked, so here I
am, like, getting driven to school by my
mom like a kid, okay? I can't wait for college next year, because I'll have a Mercedes
convertible."

Mal flicked a strand of Dawn's hair
behind her shoulder with the gun barrel,

...d she flinched. "But I know all about you," ...e said in his normal voice. "I know about that busted Ford Falcon that you ride in every day when your mom drops you off five blocks away from school. I know your father left you and your mom flat three years ago with a mountain of debt. I know your mom was on welfare for a while. And what about all those shoplifting convictions, Dawnie? How do you keep up with that wardrobe? You can't sew shoes, can you? So you just . . . walk away from the store, right?"

Dawn flinched.

"And you knew that Jamie and Greg sent letters to Denise Samarian, didn't you?" Mal crooned. "You even helped write a couple. You thought it was hysterical, didn't you? Denise thought she had a secret admirer. That's why she went to Butler's Lake that night. She was too embarrassed to admit it to the cops, wasn't she? Because she's overweight. She's fat, and she thought she had a boyfriend. You thought that was funny, didn't you?"

Dawn swallowed. "I didn't—" she whispered.

"Or maybe you just wanted Jamie think you were cool. Was that it, Princess?" Mal's voice was caressing. Dawn nodded. "And when Denise fell into the ice, and nobody came, you believed Jamie when he said he wasn't there, didn't you?" Dawn nodded again. "But you suspected him, Dawn. And you didn't break up with him, did you?" Mal ran the gun down Dawn's cheek again. She stayed rigid. "You know what that makes you, Princess? An accessory. Should I spell that word for you, hon? Is that why you were so scared when Hanigan started to nose around again?"

Dawn didn't say anything. Her body was rigid, her face a mask.

"You're a nobody, kiddo," Mal said softly, rising to his feet. He looked down at her. "You don't have money or brains. You've got blond hair—which is fake, by the way, because I saw that box in your bathroom—and blue eyes, and no personality. You've got no reason to take up space in the world, sweetheart. You're exactly the pathetic creature you think you are."

Tears filled Dawn's eyes.

"Mal, cut it out," I said.

"The prince rises to defend the lady fair," Mal said. "Even though she treats him like a worm under her feet." He stamped his foot. "Ooo, icky worm! Splat!"

"Stop it!" Dawn said fiercely. "Brian's a good guy. He's better than we are."

He held her gaze. "You think so?"

I wanted to get Mal away from Dawn. I had to keep him on track. He was focusing his anger on Dawn, and that wasn't good.

"So how come you didn't get caught, Mal?" I asked. "You didn't finish the story."

Mal turned to me. "You know the answer to that one, bud. Because no one would ever suspect me. Because I'm a nobody, too, right? And I made sure I covered my tracks. Nobody ever saw me with those guys. I didn't send those stupid e-mails back and forth. The only thing that tied me to Coach Cappy's murder was the gun."

He looked at the gun in his hand.

"That's it?" I asked.

"I still have it. That's why the guys won't rat on me. If the police had the gun, they'd be bagged for sure. Because Jamie and Greg

bought it together. They went to Dawn
part of town to do it. Did you know that it's
easy to buy a gun, Brian? No, I guess not. I
guess Jamie and Greg weren't lucky enough
to have one in the house."

I swallowed. "So they knew they were
going to kill him?"

"David tried to say they were only going
to threaten him," Mal said with a snort.
"But I don't need a lawyer to tell me that
buying a gun is a pretty good case for pre-
meditation."

"I can't believe they don't turn you in," I
said. "Why should you get off?"

He shrugged. "They have no choice.
They know that if the police had the gun,
they'd be able to trace it. And in this state,
they can all be charged with Murder One. It
doesn't matter who pulled the trigger."

"So you had all the bases covered," I
said.

"Until you messed things up," Mal said.
"That's why we had to get you out of my hair,
Brian. You were calling attention to the club.
The police realized they hadn't caught every-
one. You ruined all of it, just to get a girl."

Dawn looked up.

"Oh, you didn't know that, Princess?" Mal asked with fake concern. "So sorry to break the news. I didn't send you that key chain. *Brian* did."

"You're such a liar," Dawn said.

"I'm, like, telling the whole truth, okay?" Mal said. "Aren't I, Brian? He sent it to you to scare you. So you'd be afraid that Lobo did it. So you'd run to Brian for protection."

Dawn looked at me. Her eyes were bright with tears, and her face showed the strain. She pleaded with me with her gaze. *Tell me it's not true, Brian.*

I didn't say anything.

"So, let me think." Mal put his finger to his forehead. "Who's the bad guy here? Who's the liar? Who's the cheater?"

Dawn's head slumped down. Her shoulders shook.

"Oh, wait, one last thing, Princess," Mal said. "Don't flake out on us yet. Brian is Lobo. Not only did he try to scare you, he lied to you from the very beginning."

"How did you know I was Lobo?" I asked Mal.

"Because I have half a brain," he snarled. "Because you'd slip and use language we used together. *Eau de testosterone*, remember? But I knew before then. I knew almost from the beginning, when Lobo trashed that pitiful revue but said Dawn was the only one who could hold her head up." Mal turned to Dawn. "You stunk up the joint, sweetheart."

Dawn's voice was muffled. "What are you going to do with us?"

Mal slapped his hand on the arm of the chair, and Dawn and I jumped.

"Finally, someone gets to the point! What a surprise that it's Miss Air-for-Brains! Let me fill you in. I can't let you both go, but I have a few options."

Mal pointed the gun at me, then at Dawn.

"Unfortunately, they both involve, like, killing at least one of you, okay?"

"Wait a second," I said quickly. I didn't like the way Mal's eyes glinted. He was losing it. "You haven't told us about Emily."

"Emily." Mal sighed. "Emily. What a drag."

Dawn's voice was wobbly. "Did you kill her?"

"She caught me opening her locker," Mal said. "I was taking that other sneaker. She put the pieces together in a flash. She's smart." He frowned. "Maybe she does deserve to be valedictorian."

"How did you get her locker combination?" I asked.

Mal waved the gun. "That's no prob. I just engaged her in conversation while she was opening it. A couple of weeks ago. I was talking about you, Bri," he smirked. "The girl's got it bad. You know what she is? She's your road not taken." He turned to Dawn. "You probably don't know this, but there's this famous poet called Robert Frost? He wrote a poem called 'The Road Not Taken'—"

"I know," Dawn said. "We read it in English."

"Wow," Mal said. "You can read? Awesome. Anyway—Emily and Brian are made for each other. They're both smart. They study. They're about even in the looks department, though I'd give Emily a slight edge. Plus, Emily is truly a good person— uh, *was* truly a good person." Mal put his hand over his heart. The hand with the gun. "But you know what, Dawn? Brian didn't want Emily. She wasn't pretty enough. I mean, look at him. Do you think someone who looks like Brian has the right to make a judgment like that?"

"I don't know what you're talking about," Dawn said, shaking her head. "I want to go home."

"Of course you don't know," Mal said. "You're one of the Chosen Few! The proportions of your face—the distance between your eyes, the shape of your nose, your lips—are *pleasing*. Therefore, you will be a success in life! Does that seem fair to you, Dawn? Emily works hard for everything she gets. But because the distance between her eyes is a little too close, and her lips are a little too thin, she gets *nothing!*"

Dawn started to cry again. Helplessly, hopelessly. She shook her head back and forth, her hair falling forward.

"I didn't want to do it," Mal said to me. "Believe me. But she could have blown everything, Brian. All that detective needs is one end of the thread, and the whole ball of yarn is going to unravel. Which brings me to what to do with both of you." He whipped around. "Stop whimpering, Dawn! You're making me sick!"

She only cried harder. Mal shoved the gun barrel in her cheek.

"Mal!" I cried.

"Don't move, Brian, or I swear I'll do it," Mal said. Sweat streamed down his face. "Shut up, Dawn."

She bit her lip. She swallowed a sob. But she couldn't stop the tears.

Mal took the gun away. "Where was I?" He wiped his forehead with the hem of his T-shirt. "Okay. Okay. I'm looking at this logically. I've got a few options. Want to hear?"

Dawn and I didn't say anything.

"Number one," Mal said. "Kill both of you. Then, make it look like Brian killed Dawn, then himself. Number two—kill Dawn, leave Brian alive but plant evidence that makes him look guilty—by the way, bud, speaking of looking guilty, there's a receipt in Emily's pocket that ties you to those steroid posters, so it just might occur to the cops that you pushed her. Okay. Number three, kill Brian, make a deal with Dawn to keep her mouth shut and trust that she will. This one would be tricky. I mean, I know her popularity is important to her—but would she let me get away with murder? Which is why I just keep coming back to option number one. Both of you really have to die. Sor-ry!"

Mal leaned against the wall. His face was shiny with sweat. "It'll be quick. I mean, I'm not a monster, no matter what *some* people think."

"Mal, this is crazy, bud," I said. "You

can't kill us in cold blood. I can see panicking and giving Emily a shove—"

"So we're on the same page!" Mal cried.

"—but you couldn't just . . . shoot us!" I said.

Mal nodded. "The thing is, I could. Because I really have no choice. I don't want to go down, Brian. Look, Bigelow already suspects that you're the one who sent that memo. And I know you did. I saw you come out of Beebe's office. I was hanging posters, I heard a noise, I checked it out—I *saw* you putting those memos in the mailboxes." Mal turned to Dawn. "You didn't know your knight in shining armor did that, did you, Dawn? Did you really think that he wasn't as nasty and hypocritical as everyone else in your life? Dream on."

"Mal—"

"I'm not finished," Mal said. "You know those steroid posters? I did it. I put them up, Brian. Except I ran them off at a copy shop, and I put your name on the order. Then I tucked the copy into little dead Emily's baggy sweater pocket."

"That's not a motive," I said. "It's only a high school election, Mal."

He snorted. "In Texas, a mother her daughter's rival on the cheerlead squad, bud. Kids shoot each other ove shoes. It's a crazy world. Haven't you heard? They'll believe it. And now"—he gestured around the bunker with the gun— "there will be one more tragic event in the Bouchard bunker. Sob."

Mal looked at me sadly. "I'm sorry, bud," he said. His hand was shaking. But his aim looked pretty good to me. He walked toward me.

"Wait," I said. My voice wasn't a part of my body. I felt as if nothing went together— legs, arms, brain, fingers. Everything seemed separate and ready to break apart.

"Just close your eyes," he said. "Please." There was something deadly in his voice. He would do it. He would . . .

"NO!" Dawn screamed.

"Just look away," Mal pleaded. He placed the barrel at my temple. I could feel the gun shaking. "I can't . . . stop now. Just let me do it, man. Close your eyes. . . ."

21//you've got to have friends

"Emily is still alive!" I cried.

"You're lying," Mal said, his voice cracking. He didn't lower the gun. "Don't do it, bud. It's over."

"She is! I heard the cops talking at school. She's in a coma. What if she wakes up? Everything falls apart. But I have option number four," I said. "You don't have to take the fall."

"So to speak," Mal said. He lowered the gun slightly. "What are you saying?"

"She's alive, I swear it," I said. "But she's not expected to live past tonight. Still, can you take that chance? You can make something up about Emily. Even if by some miracle she comes to for a few seconds, even if she says your name, you can lie your way out, say you were talking, and she started to climb over, and you tried to stop he

"But she's not going to live," Mal s

"But if she *does,* and you explain
away, there's still me and Dawn. How
would you ever explain shooting two people? Accidentally? Besides, we can help
you. We can back your story up."

"The police won't know anything about
you two," Mal said. "I have a plan. And it
doesn't need to be backed up."

"If you ask me, your plan is full of
holes," I said. "Haven't you ever heard of
forensics? Do you really think you can get
away with killing us without the cops pick-
ing up one clue? You're the one who compared Hanigan to Columbo, remember? She
isn't stupid, bud. Let me point out just one
thing. Those gloves. Are you telling me that
cops can't pick up traces of powder, or
latex, on a gun barrel? Who's going to
believe that I'm out of my mind with grief
and guilt, and I shoot Dawn and myself,
and I stop to put on gloves?"

Mal looked at the gloves. Then the gun. I
saw uncertainty on his face.

"So listen to option number four," I said

ely. "It covers all the bases, and
...ody wins."

"Keep talking," Mal said.

"Okay. If you can set me up, we can set
Emily up," I said.

Mal hesitated. Dawn's sobs quieted. Her
red-rimmed eyes stayed on mine.

"Emily was unbalanced," I said. "She
was unhappy. She was obsessed with me,
right? The three of us knew that. She wrote
the steroid memo, *she* printed the posters.
When I didn't tumble for her, she decided to
frame me. She was the one who sent the key
chain and the stuffed animal to Dawn. She
was jealous, because Dawn and I were getting close."

"But Emily got a dyed sneaker," Mal
said.

"She sent it to herself," I said. "To throw
off the scent. We'll plant dye in her locker.
We'll do something. We'll figure out a way
that she could have gotten that stuffed animal. Dawn will lie about it. And Dawn and
I keep our mouths shut about tonight. I get
my presidency returned to me. Dawn goes
back to being the popular girl. And you go

back to being the smartest guy at scr.

"What if it doesn't work?" Mal a.
"I'm taking all the risks here. What if En.
wakes up?"

"That's the foolproof part of the plan," I
said. "If by some miracle things change,
we'll give you credibility, and here's the best
part: your defense attorney will be L.
Harrison Rittenhouse, Esquire. Dear old
Dad. Nothing will happen to you at all.
He'll plead insanity. Or not guilty. Or self-
defense. Doesn't matter. Because he'll get
you off. But that's just a last-case scenario.
Because it's going to work."

Mal lowered the gun further. It was
hanging at his side now. "And you two
would be accessories to murder."

"That's the beauty of it," I said. "We'll be
locked in the conspiracy. We can't betray
each other. Dawn's already an accessory to
Denise Samarian's attempted murder. She
knows something she didn't tell the cops." I
turned to Dawn. "Will you keep your
mouth shut about tonight?"

She didn't say anything for a minute.
Then, she slowly nodded. "Nothing bad

appened, right?" she said in a shaky
. "I mean, to me personally. Mal went
little crazy. So what, okay? I could definitely forget about it. Forever."

I turned back to Mal. "We want what we
had, bud," I said. "Your secret is safe.
Believe it. We've got one more year here.
Then we all go off to college. We can do it."

Mal wiped his forehead. He was sweat-
ing now. I could smell his sour perspiration.
He needed a shower. We all needed to go
home.

"What do you say, bud?" I asked softly.
"Let's do it. Let's go home. If you agree,
everybody wins. I mean, you've got to be
hungry by now. I bet there's cheesecake in
the freezer."

There was only silence in the bunker.

"I'm thinking," Mal said.

We sat there for another two hours, plan-
ning it. How to set up Emily. We went over
details so we'd all have them straight. How
Emily had a crush on me. How she'd
hounded Mal for details about me. How
once, she'd confronted Dawn and me, and

we were seriously frightened that h
on reality was slipping.

We came up with a plausible scenario
Emily getting hold of Dawn's key chain an
the stuffed animal. Mal said he had made
sure the guy at the copy shop was quitting
when he'd gotten the posters printed. No
one would be able to prove who'd placed
that order for sure.

It was all lies, but it all hung together.
The trick was, it was the three of us. As long
as we would hang together, we could do it.

And slowly, as the hours ticked on, something strange happened. We got closer. In
every way. We started out with Mal leaning
against the wall, Dawn in the chair, me in
the middle of the room. By the time we'd
finished, we were sitting in a circle on the
floor, our knees touching, our eyes meeting.

For the first time since I'd started high
school, I felt like I belonged to something.
Sure, it was an evil conspiracy. But, hey, I
was bonding with my peers at last.

Afterward, we went to Mal's house. I
called my dad and explained what had happened at school. How I'd been minding my

...siness when I'd heard the noise of
...thing falling. How I'd looked out the
...dow and had seen Emily lying below.
...ow Hanigan thought I'd done it, so I'd
run. It was stupid, but I needed help.

Dad came and picked me up. Dawn and
Mal went with me to the police station. Dad
felt we should all tell Detective Hanigan
how erratically Emily had been behaving.
We pretended to be reluctant, but we'd
already rehearsed everything. We were pre-
pared.

Detective Hanigan let Dad tell her how
I'd come upon the scene, and why I'd run,
"just like any normal teenager, considering
the circumstances."

Dad gave Hanigan his most lawyerly
look, all folksy and sincere and *aren't we on
the same side, here?*

"After what happened last year, you can't
blame Brian—though he was wrong, of
course!—for panicking, and thinking that
the police would find another Bloomfield
student guilty of murder—"

"Murder?" Hanigan asked. "I wasn't
going to arrest Brian for murder, Mr.

Rittenhouse. I just wanted to question him. Besides, a murder charge isn't being considered for anyone—yet. Emily Talladega is still alive."

"How is the young girl doing?" Dad asked in a concerned tone.

"Not well," Hanigan said. She kept her eyes on us. "She's not expected to make it."

We all looked appropriately sad. I could feel the current running between us. We were together. We were pulling it off. We could do anything.

It was only later, after my dad got me released, after the lecture he gave me in the car on the way home, after the lights were out and I was safe in my own bed, that I realized what I'd done.

I'd felt relief that someone might die.

Emily, who'd never done anything to me except be as smart as I was and have the nerve to like me, even though she was a Never.

I'd wanted her to die.

Suddenly, horror rose in my throat like a choke hold. Every breath was tainted with bile, because *I still wanted her to die.*

I found myself on my knees. I don't even remember slipping out of bed. There I was, like a little kid, my forehead against the mattress. I hadn't done this in years and years.

But I couldn't pray. That option was closed to me now. I had crossed the line. I had touched evil and, bit by bit, I had taken evil inside me.

But at least I had friends.

epilogue

Subj: *Seasons Greetingz*
Date: *Monday*
From: *LoneLobo*

Sleigh bells ring, are you listening? The Yuletide season is upon us, and Lobo can't wait for New Year's. It's taken months for all of us to get over Emily's tragic attempted suicide. We're all still pulling for her recovery, and Lobo suggests that remembering her with a card at the hospital would be a gesture. Yeah, I know she's still coma-bound, but her parents deserve our support.

The lesson learned: If you ever get that desperate, people, go to a shrink. Or Bermuda. Throwing yourself on concrete is not an option, and just think what it does to your hair.

Our newest and grooviest Fun Couple, Prez Brian Rittenhouse and Head Cheerleader Dawn Sedaris (an Odd Couple, but hey, they work it!) are throwing a bash to end all bashes at former nerdling Mal Bouchard's palatial digs. If you're wondering if Lobo is invited, Lobo very much is— I'll be watching and listening, so play nice, boyz and grrrlz.

Just a parting note. Not to be a downer. But while the Coach Cappy trial drags on, and Emily sleeps, Lobo has been thinking.

This school may be the best in the state, just like we keep telling each other. But the forces that drove Emily and the jocks didn't spring out of nowhere. They came out of something dark. Something we didn't want to see.

Lobo has seen it, my friends. I've touched it. Maybe I've even been it. I know how close the darkness is.

So here's my Christmas message to all of you at Bloomfield High:

Love Your Hair. But Watch Your Backs.

I swung by Dawn's locker at the end of the

school day. She was reaching for a b
and I came up from behind and kissed
back of her head. I still couldn't believe w
were together.

She flinched, then turned. "Oh, it's you."

"Ready to split? We've got tons of plan-
ning for the party. I thought we'd go down-
town for the decorations. Krandalls has the
best ones," I said. I totally dug going places
with Dawn. Everyone always turned and
looked. They wondered how a nerd like me
could snag such a knockout.

"Yeah, I guess." Dawn sighed. "I have so
much homework."

"I'll do it for you," I said.

She looked irritated. "You know, Brian,
you really don't have to keep offering to do
everything I don't want to do."

"I just want you to be happy," I said.

"Yeah," she said. "Constantly." She
slammed her locker shut. She wound this
awesome scarf I'd bought her around her
neck. It matched her dark blue eyes. Then
she shrugged into her coat.

I knew that behind my back, Dawn's
crowd called me "Smother Love." And

be I got on Dawn's nerves sometimes. I
ot giving her presents, and doing her
omework for her, and generally trying to
make her life easier.

There were dark rings of shadows under
her eyes now. She had cut her hair, and
sometimes she forgot to touch up her roots.
Her golden beauty had dimmed a tad. But I
didn't care.

I had a few bad nights myself. But then
when I came to school, I was president of
the student body, and Dawn Sedaris was my
girlfriend, and I was okay again.

Hanigan poked around for way longer
than was comfortable. A couple of months,
in fact. She'd just kept asking questions.
Then I'd call my dad, and he'd do some
lawyerly thing, and slap her down. She
hadn't been around in weeks, and it had
been a pleasure.

Poor Hanigan. Maybe I could buy her a
basket of those gourmet coffees for
Christmas.

Mal was the only one of us who wasn't
bothered by sleepless nights, or twinges of
guilt. He had applied for early admission to

Dartmouth, and it looked like he was ?
get in. He wouldn't even finish out senio.

Which made me relieved, to tell you
truth. Mal and I weren't such good bud
anymore. As a matter of fact, we avoided
each other now. I think he'd offered to have
this party at his house just to meet girls. He
wanted Dawn and me to host it so that
everyone would come. And we knew we
had to say yes.

We all had to say yes to each other.
Which made me wonder sometimes what
the real reason was that Dawn never broke
up with me. She snapped at me, fought with
me, and barely let me kiss her. But she never
told me to get lost.

I didn't want to know why she didn't
break up with me. I just wanted to be with
her. I wanted to be a couple. I only felt a
tiny atom of peace when I was touching
Dawn.

"I don't know why Mal doesn't buy the
decorations," Dawn grumbled as we headed outside into the cold air. "It's really his
party. And it took us hours yesterday to do
all those invitations."

...d we'd do it," I said. I took her ... but she dropped mine a second later to ... on her gloves. I pretended not to notice. ...After all, he's taking care of all the food."

The sky was the bright, sharp blue it gets when it's near freezing. The sun was so bright, I felt dazzled. The snow was a pristine white blanket covering the school grounds. It was a picture-perfect day at a picture-perfect school.

This is the way life is for everyone else, only I never knew it, I thought. *It was worth it.* The nightmares would go away. Slowly. But they'd go. I didn't have one last night. Not one. I took Dawn's hand again.

Heidi Huberman came running out of school. She wasn't wearing a coat, and she was laughing. Bloomfield was getting more full of psychos every day.

"What's with Heidi?" I asked.

"Maybe she just got her invitation," Dawn said sourly. "It's probably the only party she's ever been invited to."

Heidi rushed up to us, her cheeks pink and glowing. "Did you hear? Did you hear the news?"

"What news?" I asked.

"Emily came out of her coma!" ˌsquealed. "She's talking! She's going tⱱ all right! I'm going there right now!"

She sprinted off toward the parking lot. We stopped and watched until her legs twinkled in the distance. She was wearing hiking boots and red tights. The color looked like a splash of blood against the snow.

The world seemed to drop away in front of my eyes. Level ground suddenly tilted downhill. The sun glinted off the whiteness and hit my eyes like a nuclear blast.

I felt Dawn's fingers slip from my grasp. Her moan seemed to come to me from far away, and suddenly, I was alone.

1//blown away

Let me start off by giving you a critical piece of advice for your future—never, under any circumstances, allow yourself to be trapped in a room with five girls and a pile of baby pictures.

"Ooooo! Look at Jason! He's soooooo cute!" Desi Radowitz crooned.

"Eeeeee! Check out Bobby Harrison!" Jessica Rabin let out a high–pitched squeal and tossed the photo to Sarah Grommet.

"Eeeeee!" Sarah squealed.

I checked to see if the classroom windows had shattered. They hadn't.

I had volunteered to help organize baby photos of the junior class for the yearbook and write funny captions for each of them. Now the question was why, why, why?

"Can we get organized here?" I suggested.

"Maybe we should alphabetize—"

"Ewwwwwww!"

I just about jumped to the ceiling. But ~~it was~~
only Winona Bede who'd come up behind m~~e~~.

"Look at Josh Towney! He looks like a monkey!" Winona cried.

I had this tiny sensitivity to loud noises and
shrieks. If someone creeps up behind me and
goes boo, I go into cardiac arrest. It was one of
those embarrassing things about yourself that
you don't want anyone to know.

Jessica snatched the photo back. "He does
not! He's cute!"

"Eewwwwww," Winona repeated.

"Let me see!" Sarah demanded.

"Hey!" I tried. "We've been here for twenty
minutes already, and we haven't even—"

"Eeeeeee! He does look like a monkey!"

Let me stop right here. I'm not dissing girls.
These girls were not airheads. They were all
probably smarter than me. But get a bunch of
girls around baby pictures, and what do you
get? Mayhem.

Even my best friend, Sydney Gross, was giggling over the pictures. And Syd was not the giggling type.

She held up a picture of Brad Winkler, junior
class would-be stud. "Look at this one. Proof

er really is a hound in guy disguise."

...l looked at the photo and burst out —
...ng. Baby Brad was a pudgy tyke with the
...e long face and blond curly hair. He was on
...n fours, and had a ball in his mouth.

Jessica looked up from the picture of Brad.
"Hey, where's your picture, MacFarland?"

I pushed over my picture to her. My mom
had dug it up out of a pile she kept in a drawer.
I had bought her a photo album for Christmas
two years ago, and she still hadn't gotten around
to putting all her photos in it. Mom was super
organized at her business, but our house?
Chaos.

When I'd asked for a picture of myself as a
baby, Mom had dug into this overstuffed drawer to find her favorite. I guess I was around four
or five years old. I had a baseball mitt on one
hand that was almost as big as I was. In my
other hand was a stuffed dog I'd named
"Pokey."

Jessica widened her green eyes at me. "Do
you miss your yittle stuffed puppy?" she asked
in baby talk.

"What are you talking about? I still sleep
with him. Every night," I said. Jessica was a
goon. But she had coppery hair and some
wicked long legs, and all I wanted from life at

the moment was to sit next to her ⟨
and watch her cross them.

Syd glanced at the picture. "You're p⟨
here, Andy," she said. "Everybody else is a
and you're almost in school."

"It's symbolic of how incredibly more matur⟨
I am than all you guys," I said.

Jessica snorted. "I hope you enjoy being
delusional, MacFarland."

"Yeah, dream on," Desi said.

"Really, Andy," Syd said. "Doesn't your
mom have any pictures of you as a baby?"

I thought about it. Baby pictures were not
high on my agenda. The earliest picture I could
remember was me on the first day of kinder-
garten. Mom was not exactly a shutterbug. She
always forgot to buy film, or misplaced the cam-
era.

"Don't you have a baby book?" Winona
asked me. "My mom filled this book with pictures of me, and wrote down things like the first
time I smiled, or stood up, or ate my first piece
of broccoli...."

"Just don't get into potty training, okay?"
Syd said. "I think baby books are goony."

"I have one," Jessica said.

"I have one, too," Desi said. "Except it's only
got like, three pages filled out, because my mom

. m the fifth kid. That's what hap-
, families. The youngest one gets left

o wonder you need therapy," Syd said.
. rolled her eyes.

We started to organize the photos and think of captions. But only half of my brain was paying attention. It was like this little noise was pinging in my head. Why weren't there any baby pictures of me around the house? Maybe Mom had been too tired to take any. My dad had left about five months after I was born—nice guy, huh? We hadn't heard from him since.

So Mom had raised me alone pretty much from day one. But suddenly, I started wondering about whether she'd wanted me or not. Her husband left her because she had a baby. He couldn't handle the responsibility—or the noise. What if she really resented me?

Whoa. Now *I* needed therapy.

* * *

"Mom, where can I find baby pictures of me?"

After the meeting, I tracked Mom down in her office Maybe I shouldn't say "tracked," as if it were hard. Mom was always in her office. It was five o'clock, and she'd probably still be here for another hour. Mom was partners with

Syd's mom, Rachel, in this busir̶̶
Yellow Crayon. They made CD–rom g̶̶
girls. They were super busy at the momen̶̶
Mom was always home for dinner—even if
had to go back to the office afterward.

Mom looked up. She blinked at me in slow
motion. I guess I'd interrupted her train of
thought.

"Baby pictures," she repeated.

"Yeah," I said. I leaned a hip against her desk
"We're putting baby pictures of ourselves in the
yearbook, remember? The one you gave me was
too old. Don't you have one of me when I was
little? You know, like, crawling?"

"What's wrong with the one I gave you?"
Mom asked. "It's my favorite. You look so
cute—"

"I'm just way older than everybody else," I
said.

Mom looked down at her papers. She
frowned. Then, she looked out the window. "I
don't have any pictures of you as a baby," she
said softly.

I let out a long breath. "Oh. Look, we don't
have to get all psychological here, okay? But did
you...want me?"

Mom looked at me then She has very clear,
very bright blue eyes. There were tears in them.

you more than anything in the world,

then why didn't you take pictures of me?" ...ked. "Or have a stupid baby book? Was it ...cause Todd left you? Did you think it was my fault?"

"My husband was an idiot," Mom said, pushing at a drawer that was already closed. "That's why he left."

"So why—"

"Andy." Mom dropped her head in her hands. She took a deep breath. Then she looked up. But she didn't look at me. She looked out the window. Her office was in an old house, and there was a backyard with a big, leafy tree. She stared at it.

"I've been debating with myself about telling you something," she said. "Something you should know. It's just that I hate to...I told myself that it wasn't something you needed to know...."

She was fumbling, but I didn't say anything. Suddenly, I was very, very scared. Because she looked scared.

She turned and looked at me. "You have to understand how much I love you," she said, her voice wobbly. "When you love someone, when you love your child, the first duty you have is to protect him. It goes deeper than thinking—it's instinct. That's why I waited—"

"Mom! You are truly freaking me out," I said. "Will you just cut to the chase?"

"You're adopted," she said.

Suddenly, there was no floor under my feet. "What?"

"I adopted you," she said. "When you were three years old."

The news trickled down inside me like icy rain. I couldn't move. A gust of wind sent the papers flying. That's when the image of snow came to me. A blizzard, flying in my face, biting into me with cold fingers.

"But...wait," I said. "What happened to my real parents?"

I saw Mom flinch at the word "real." But I didn't care.

"Your mother died," she said. Her gaze slid away from mine.

There was more. I knew it. I knew she didn't want to tell me. My face felt hot, and my whole body had started to shake.

"How did she die?" I demanded. "Where was my father? What happened to him?"

She didn't answer.

I pounded on her desk with my fists. "Tell me!"

"He killed her," she whispered.